For my wife Lisa

There was you
When I was getting countless rejection letters,
There was you
When I was filled with bouts of self-doubt,
There was you
When I needed someone to lean on and encourage me
There was you
You have been with me on my darkest day and in my shining
hour
Without you, none of this would be possible
You've been so good to me, even on the days I didn't deserve it.
For your continuous, and at times unwavering support of me,
I dedicate the first book in this series to you.
All my love,
Your husband,
Cornelius

Chapter One

Beck and Jazz are in a car driving down a one-way street. Beck is a young man of about twenty-two years old. Jazz is seventeen years old. Beck is driving, and Jazz is riding shotgun. Both are very unkempt with nappy, knotty hair, dirty fingernails, and old clothes.

"What about up this block? Did we go up this block before?" Beck says.

Jazz looks out his side of the window then looks and Beck and says, "Why are we even out here? If we go back now, we can still catch that movie on streaming. Why can't we do that?"

Beck gives him a quick glance before looking back out the window scanning the street. "Do you realize how gay that sounds"? He says.

"You don't have to be such a homophobe." Jazz says.

"A homo-who?" Beck replies confused. He points to a building on the side. "There they are." He says. Beck slows the car down in front of a building with a few people standing in front of it. He rolls the window down. One man, Kevin moves closer to the car and says, "Yo Beck! What up?" Beck smiles and says, "S'up Kev? What's going on?"

"I ain't seen you in a minute. Where you been?" Kevin asks. Beck smiles and says, "Here and there. You got something for me?" "You know I do." Kevin says back.

Beck says, "Let me get a parking spot, and I'll be right there." "Cool! I think there's one up the street over there." Kevin replies while pointing up the street.

Beck closes the window and moves slowly up the street until he sees a vacant parking spot. He begins to back up into it. "What were we talking about before?" Beck asks. Jazz turns to him and says, "I said you sound like a homophobe."

"Yeah. What the hell is that? Beck asks very confusedly.

Jazz looks him in the face and says, "A homophobe. It's a person who has a strong dislike for homosexuals."

Beck turns to look at Jazz and says, "Where the fuck do you get this shit?"

Jazz looks back out his side of the window. "From the news." He says.

Beck snaps, "Stop watching the news. All that shit is fake."

Beck tries to park the car but almost hits the car in front of him. He pulls out of the spot and tries again. "You can't even park this." Jazz says.

"Shut up. I'm concentrating." Beck says sternly. He lines up the car and backs slowly into the spot. Beck smiles and nudges Jazz.

"Congratulations." Jazz says.

Beck turns off the car and they both get out and walk toward Kevin and his crew.

"Are they in on it? Kevin and his crew?" Jazz asks. Becks looks at him and says, "I don't think so. All they said we have to do is lure him out. If we see him, we run across to the projects and head up to the roof, and they will take care of the rest." Jazz looks around and says, "Which roof? Is that where they are?"

Beck looks around also. "Not sure. They didn't want to say too much because they didn't want him to become suspicious."

Jazz stops Beck from walking. "And why the fuck are we doing this?" Jazz demands. Beck moves closer to him and says, "Cause we have no choice. Look, I don't want to be here either, but we have to do this, right? We bring him out of his cave, they take him in, we get some stuff and go back to the crib, and we'll watch whatever you want on streaming, OK? And it won't be homophobic at all. It won't even be the least bit gay." Jazz says, "The least bit gay?" Jazz smiles at Beck. Beck hits him. "Whatever man. Let's do this."

They both approach Kevin and his gang. They all exchange greetings with handshakes and half hugs.

Kevin moves closer to Beck and says, "Yo, I thought Russell told you to stay outta this neighborhood cause this was his area now."

"You know what? Fuck him. Fuck Russell. He ain't running anything. He don't tell me what to do." Beck says. "But we can't stay long. We need some stuff so we can be on our way." "You got money?" Kevin asks. Beck takes out a wad of cash and says, "Of course I do. I'll take the usual stuff."

Kevin goes into the building vestibule where his bag is. Suddenly an unmarked police car with light flashing comes up the wrong way of the one-way street they're on. Kevin looks at the car and says, "Shit!" They all scatter. Russell gets out of the car and stares menacingly at Beck and Jazz. He is a white male in his late thirties and quite overweight. His eyes are wide, his nostrils are flaring, and he's breathing heavy. Jazz looks at Russell's enraged face and says, "Fuck!!" They both run and Russell yells out, "Don't fucking make me chase after you!" Seeing they are not stopping, Russell gives chase.

They run until they reach the nearby projects. Jazz yells at Beck, "Which building?" Beck points to one and says, "Over here!" They both run into a building with Russell hot on their heels.

In the lobby, Jazz and Beck get to the elevator and sees the door is already open. They both go inside and press the top floor. They hear his footsteps coming closer and louder. Jazz yells, "We're going to die!" Beck presses the top floor button very hard multiple times and yells, "Let's go! What the fuck!" An old woman comes out of the stairwell and walks past them saying, "The elevator's been out for a week honey." Just them, they see Russell enter the building. He yells, "Motherfucker!" They leave the elevator and burst open the stairwell door and race up the stairs.

In the stairwell, Beck is in front running top speed. Jazz occasionally looks down and sees Russell's hand on the railing to see where he is. "He's getting closer! Hurry the fuck up, man!!" He yells.

Beck gets to the rooftop breathing very heavy. He looks around and doesn't see anyone. Jazz soon follows and is also breathing very heavy. He is also looking around. He grabs Beck and yells, "Where the fuck are they? I thought you said they'd be here." They both hear the footsteps coming closer up the stairs. They both look at each other. Jazz says, "What do we do?" Beck looks at him with a terrified expression on his face.

Russell finally reaches the rooftop. He is breathing very heavy and has veins bulging out of his neck. Russell punches Jazz in the face so hard; he breaks his nose. Jazz falls back and grabs his nose. "Fuck!!!" He yells.

Russell takes out his gun and says to Jazz, "That's for making me run." He shoots Jazz in his chest, and he falls dead. "And that's for coming around here." Russell says through his heavy breathing. He moves closer to Beck and points his gun at Beck's head. Beck gets down on his knees and cowers in a corner on the rooftop. "What the fuck are you doing around here? Didn't I say to stay out of this area?" Russell asks. Beck keeps his head down and his hands up and says, "Yo man please! Don't shoot! Please don't shoot!" Russell moves closer to Beck and says, "What the fuck were you guys doing around here anyway?"

"Look, we were getting some stuff and taking it back to my house. That's it." Beck says.

"Get up." Russell says.

Beck puts his head down and says with his voice quivering, "Please don't kill me. I swear I'll never set foot in this area again. Just please don't kill me."

"I said get the fuck up!" Russell says again. Beck slowly puts his hands down and stands up with his head still down.

"Look at me." Russell says.

Beck slowly directs his eyes to Russell's face. Russell takes a step towards Beck, and he jumps back. Russell says, "If you want to live, get rid of this body and clean this mess up. I'll get you some help with this. You do that, and we're cool. You got it?" Beck looks Russell in the eye and smiles a little and says, "Don't worry. I-I'll take care of it." Russell goes back into the stairwell.

He gets halfway down the stairs when he takes out his phone and makes a call. "Hey. I need a cleanup crew over here in the projects. It's on the roof. I think I'm in building four. No, I can't be here to help out. I have an awards ceremony to go to. No, not for me you asshole. Who else?"

*

The Simms family live in a modest two-family semi-attached house in the Pelham Parkway section of the Bronx. The home sits on the corner of Astor and Bronxwood Ave. Along Astor Ave from Boston Road to Bronxwood is a large Albanian population. On either side of the street, there are Albanian businesses and other shops. They mostly keep to themselves talking in groups on the corner and smoking lots of cigarettes. This influx of people has given the area and unique nickname. In the upstairs bedroom is Tom Simms. He's a middle-aged white male with salt and pepper hair. Tom is putting on a very nice crisp white dress shirt. He then goes to his side of the closet and picks out a tie to match his blue suit. He ties the knot and puts on his suit jacket. Tom stands in front of a full-length mirror and takes a long look at himself. He takes a deep breath and puts on his wedding ring and leaves.

Tom goes downstairs where he sees his wife Amy and daughter Sabrina. Amy is about fifteen years younger than Tom. She has long brown hair and brown eyes. Sabrina is a seventeen-year-old teenager. She is texting on her phone. Neither one is dressed to go anywhere. Amy is sitting at the kitchen table smoking a cigarette looking a lot of papers in front of her. Tom stands in front of with his arms out and says, "So? How do I look?" Amy doesn't look up, so Tom moves a little closer to her.

"Amy!" He says a little louder. Amy finally looks up at him. "What do you think?" He asks.

"You look fine." Amy mumbles then she goes back to looking at her papers. Tom turns and to Sabrina with his arms out, but she continues to text never looking up for a second. He puts his arms down, waves Sabrina off and walks over to Amy and says, "Is there any way I could convince you guys to come?"

Amy almost slams down the paper she was reading and says, "We went over this already. Remember?"
"I know." Tom says. "But this is not the first ceremony you haven't attended. We haven't been seen together in public for a good while, and people are starting to think we have problems." He continues.

Amy slams her fist down the table and yells, "We are having problems!" Sabrina finally looks up from her phone and walks over to her parents. Amy shuffles the papers in front of her and says, "There is so much going wrong in our lives right now. You see all of these papers? These are estimates from the plumber, roofer and the dentist. I'm supposed to get a call later tonight and find out how much all of this is going to cost us."

Sabrina looks over at Tom and says, "You also promised to teach me how to drive. When are you going to start doing that?" Tom walks over to her and tries to put a reassuring hand on her shoulder, but Sabrina backs away a little. "Look, after I retire, I can devote more time to both of you, and we can do all the things we said we would." Tom says.

"Well, even after Sabrina gets her license, that car is way too old for her to drive." Amy responds.

Tom turns in Amy's direction and says, "What are you talking about? The car runs great!"

"That car is so old; it doesn't even have a backup camera." Amy says.

"But the car has so much horsepower. It has four-wheel drive and heated seats." Tom counters back.

She now stands up and says, "Meanwhile Debbie just bought a new Mercedes SL Class Roadster. She's also been asking for us to come out there for lunch, but I've been stalling."

"Stalling? Why?" asks Tom.

Amy turns her eyes away and says, "Because I didn't think we can afford it."

Tom walks over to her and holds her in his arms and says, "Honey. We can afford lunch." She pushes him away and yells, "I don't want lunch! I want a new fucking house!   I hate where I live, and I hate the Bronx! All these fucking people do is eat Burek and smoke. And what the fuck is Burek anyway? I hate how they try to squeeze into small seats on the five train. They always sit with their arms crossed like they own something and they all get off at fifty-ninth street. Do they all work in the same company? You know what they call this area now? They call it Albania Alley. That's how many of them are here. You've got the niggers from the projects on the left and the niggers from Europe on the right, and I'm stuck in the middle with you. Isn't the president supposed to get rid of these people?"

Tom stares at her for a minute not believing what she just said. Finally, he says, "Only if they're here illegally."

Amy walks over to the fridge and opens a beer. She takes a sip and says, "I'm sure some of them swam over here."

"I doubt they swam from Albania." Tom responds back.

"We should really talk about moving out to Long Island. At least there are no Albanians out there." Amy says.

Tom looks her in the face and says, "Uhh I'm pretty sure there are Albanians on the Island too."

Amy take another swig of her beer and says, "Yeah, but at least they are the good kind." Tom shakes his head and starts to go upstairs. "You know." Amy says, and Tom stops at the bottom of the stairs. "The house near Debbie and Russ is for sale. We should at least take a look at it." Amy continues.

Tom now walks toward her again and says, "We can't afford a new house. We are still trying to make repairs on this one."

"Well, Russ hasn't on the job as long as you and they have a really nice house." Amy says to Tom.

Tom moves closer to Amy and says, "Russ is also under investigation from Internal Affairs."

"Really? For what?" Amy asks.

Tom turns away a little and says, "Not sure, but if IA is watching you, it's usually not a good thing."

Amy takes another sip of her beer and says, "He's getting it done."

"Did you hear what I said? He's doing something illegal!" Tom says raising his voice.

Amy finishes her beer, throws the bottle in the recycling bin and says, "Did you hear what I said? He's still getting it done."

Tom looks at Amy and shakes his head again. He checks his watching and says, "I have to go." He goes upstairs to finish getting dressed. Amy looks at the clock on the wall and mumbles, "Whatever." She takes out another beer from the fridge and sits back down to look at all the papers in front of her.

*

In a vast hall, Tom is standing with about seven other officers. They are holding up their awards and having their picture taken by the press. The officers' families are also taking pictures. After the pictures are finished being taken, the officers congratulate each other for their perspective awards. The officers then separate and then join their families for private pictures. Tom slinks away and watches an officer pose for pictures with his wife and teenage daughter. Off in the distance, Tom sees Russell walking in his direction looking very nervous. He shakes Tom's hand.

"Hey, Russ! Surprised to see you here." Tom says with a smile.

Russ smiles back and says, "Yeah, I was never invited to these things, so I decided to crash." Russ looks around for a bit. "Where's Amy? I didn't see her." He asks.

The smile goes away from Tom's face, and he mutters, "Oh she couldn't make it tonight."

"You know, Debbie wanted to get together for lunch with Amy, but she said she couldn't make that either. Is everything OK with you guys?" Russ asks.

Tom looks away slightly and says, "Yeah. Everything is fine, but we have a lot on our plates right now. The house needs lots of repairs, and she's been dealing with that for the most part." Tom notices Russ' nervousness and asks, "What's the matter?" Tom moves a little closer to Russ and asks, "Hey, did they ever find that gun you say you lost? Sorry, but was it lost or stolen?"

Russ frowns at him a little and states, "As I told them, I was chasing a perp, and it must have fallen out."

"And how long ago was that? Tom asks. "Shit, that was almost four months ago." Russ replies.

"And no new leads on that case?" Tom asks.

"Not yet." Russ says. "But I have a pretty good idea where it might be. But I have more pressing things on my mind." He continues.

"Like what?" Tom asks. Russ motions over his shoulder and points to Detectives Gibbons and Lars. Both are staring at Russ very intently.

"IA is still sniffing around you, huh?" Tom wonders. "They've been on my ass for years. They really wanted my old partner and not me." Russ says.

Tom pulls Russ to the side and says, "You mean the one who resigned in disgrace? He also lost his pension and did a little time because – "

"Bullshit! There are two sides to every story you know?" Russ exclaims cutting Tom off and pushing him up against the wall. Tom pushes him back and says, "Don't get familiar with me." Russ backs up a little and says, "I'm sorry, but it upsets me when—"

"How is Jason by the way? I heard he's in a wheelchair now?" Tom says interrupting Russ back.

"Yeah, he was shot." Russ replies. Russ looks away and looks down. Tom moves a little closer to Russ and asks, "What it a hit?"

"Not sure. We think so, but we're not sure. We never found out who did it." Russ replies.

Gibbons and Lars slowly walk over to Russ and Tom. As they approach, Russ looks increasingly nervous. He adjusts his stance and readies himself. Gibbons and Lars both smile and Tom and give him a very hearty handshake.

"Congratulations Tom." Lars says. "Is it true you are retiring in about a year?"

Tom smiles slightly and says, "More or less. That's my timeline. I need to focus on my family."

Gibbons steps forward a little and says, "We all wish there were a way to convince you to stay on the job a little longer."

"Really? Why?" Tom inquires.

Gibbons looks him straight in the eye and says, "Well, you are one of the most highly treasured cops on the force. You are a positive inspiration to all, and you are a constant beacon of light to other cops whose moral compass has them lost with no hope of salvation." He then turns to turns to Russell pretending he hadn't noticed him before and says, "Oh, hey Russ. Didn't see you standing there."

"Gibbons." Russ replies dryly.

Lars walks a little closer to him and asks, "What are you doing here? Did you get an award too?"

"No. I just stopped by to talk to Tom here. That's all." Russ replies.

Lars stares at Russ for a bit before Gibbons steps toward Russ to shake Tom's hand again and says, "Congratulations Tom. Very well deserved." He then looks at Lars, tugs on his jacket slightly and says, "Let's go." Lars shakes Tom's hand again, gives Russ a little side eye before they both walk away.

Russ looks at them walk away, then turns to Tom and asks, "Assholes got nothing better to do?" He looks at his watch and says, "Look, Tom, if you ever want to run the streets with me, all you have to do is ask. I think we'd make a great team. Think about it." Russ walks away.

Tom's phone rings. He takes it out and sees Amy is calling him. He starts to answer but decided to let it go to voicemail.

Detective Baker, a middle-aged black man, walks over to him with a smile on his face as he shakes Tom's hand. "Just when I thought you couldn't possibly top an already stellar career, you surprise us all over again!" Baker exclaims.

"Baker! How the hell are you?" Tom asks. "Keeping busy. Trying to put as many assholes off the street as possible." Baker responds back. "Really? You got something cooking now?" Tom asks.

Baker walks a little closer to Tom and whispers, "Well, I have a little operation that's about to go down later tonight." Tom's eyes widen and says, "No shit! Tonight?" "And I was wondering if NYPD's most decorated officer wanted to tag along and observe." Baker says.

The smile on Tom's face slowly fades away. "I—I don't know." Tom says. "I really should get home. I have a lot going on right now. I'm not sure if I should." Tom takes out his phone and says, "Amy left me a message."

Baker says, "Check the message. If it's urgent, then go home and take care of your business. If not, then come hang with us."

Tom checks his voicemail from Amy. Her message says, "While you're there getting another fucking award for a job well done, I'm here taking care of shit that really matters! Where the fuck are you? I got the estimates and did the math, and everything's going to cost fifteen thousand dollars. Did you hear what I just said? Fifteen thousand dollars! How the fuck are we going to pay for this? I don't know where you are, but you need to call me back so we can talk about how you're gonna handle this shit! And Debbie left me another message saying Russell came by to see you today. What did you tell him? Are we getting together for lunch? What the fuck—" Tom hangs up his phone to find Baker staring at him.

"Well?" Baker asks. Tom looks at him, draws a slight smile and says, "Let's go."

Chapter Two

Baker and Tom walk down a hallway in an apartment building. They get to a particular door, and Baker knocks. An officer opens the door to let them in. Inside the apartment, there's a large group of police officers scattered around. Some are sitting at a large kitchen table with technical equipment, and other officers are wearing bulletproof vests on the outside of their shirts with their badges around their necks. As soon as Tom walks in the living room area, the cops all break out in spontaneous applause. Some of the officers walk over to shake his hand. Tom waves them all off and slightly smiles and looks at the ground. Baker puts his arm around Tom and says, "You guys knock it off. You're embarrassing him. Get back to work!" Baker leads Tom to the audio surveillance area.

"What's the sit-rep?" Tom asks.

"I have a pigeon named Angel who is very close to leading us to a huge fish" Baker responds. "How big a fish?" Tom asks.

Baker looks Tom in the eye and says, "Clayton." Tom's mouth slightly drops.

"No one has seen him in person in years. Some cops even said he wasn't real. Just a made-up name to throw us cops off. A few months ago, there was a robbery at a pawn shop. It rained a lot that day, and we caught a break. There were boot prints that were confirmed to be his. Cameras didn't catch his face though. All the leads dried up, so we thought someone just put his boots on and pretended to be Clayton." Baker says. "You thought it was a hoax?" Tom asks. "We did for a long time until a few weeks ago with the Brink's job." Baker responds back. Tom looks at Baker and shakes his head. "You mean Francis Brink?" Tom asks. "Yup." Baker continues. "Brink was a top kingpin. He had connections all over the city. We were close to getting him but someone in his crew set him up, and there was a violent shoot out."

"That's right! There were bodies and blood all over the place." Tom replies. "The bodies were easy to identify, but it took weeks for the lab to bring back the blood results. His blood was mixed in with others, and there was no positive ID. So, the techs went back to the crime scene and there it was. A single drop of his blood separated from everyone else. That one drop of blood was the one break we needed." Baker exclaims.

"No shit!" Tom yells.

"We had the lab test it several times just to confirm, and it is Clayton's blood. We had him. You couldn't fake that. That's his first confirmed appearance in months. We've been after him ever since." Baker says.

"I know. You've been after him for a while." Tom mentions.

"And tonight, we get one step closer to catching him." Baker says. "And how do you know this guy will talk?" Tom asks.

"Oh. He'll fucking talk. Trust me." Baker affirms with authority. "And which one has direct contact with Clayton?" Tom asks. Baker goes over to a few sheets of paper with information on it. He picks up one sheet and says, "This is the one. Let me see. Uhh someone named Gamble. He has direct contact. He brought two guys as a backup, but Gamble is the one we need."

Detective Smalls comes over to Baker and says, "Your rat needs a thicker pair of socks." Baker rolls his eyes and sighs deeply. Tom looks at Baker very confused. Baker turns to Tom and says, "My guy is getting cold feet." They all make their way to the surveillance table where Angel's mic is.

"What's his fucking problem, now?" Baker asks.

"Not sure. He keeps mumbling about Smiley being there and not knowing he was coming. You need to talk him off this ledge. It's almost showtime." Smalls warns.

Baker goes over to the microphone directly to Angel. "Angel." Baker whispers.

"W-Where the fuck are you?" Angel says in between heavy breathing. "I'm close by. What's the matter? Where are you?" Baker asks.

"I'm in the b-bathroom. You didn't tell me Smiley was here." Angel says with panic in his voice. Baker asks, "Who the fuck is Smiley?"

"He's someone you don't fuck with. He don't hesitate." Angel exclaims.

Baker picks up the microphone and explains, "Look, everything is in place. All you have to make the deal. Once it's done, we'll swoop in, arrest them all, including this Smiley person and you're good to go."

"Oh man. I don't know man. Smiley kinda changes things." Angel says.

"This doesn't change shit." Baker says with his voice rising. Other officers indicate to Baker non-verbally he should lower his voice. Baker takes a deep breath and mutters under gritted teeth, "Look, we've all come too far to turn back now. You said you had enough and wanted out of this life, right? Well, this is how you do it. Just grow a pair of balls for five minutes. That's it. Where's Gamble?"

There is loud banging on the bathroom door. "Yo, Angel! What the fuck are you doing in there? Let's do this!" A voice says. Baker holds the mic close to his mouth and says, "Now get out there. Stay calm and do your thing. You can do this." "I'll be right out Milo." Angel yells. Baker grabs a pen and writes Milo and Smiley on a piece of paper.

The officers who are listening hears the bathroom door open. "Sorry, guys I was taking a shit." Angel says.

"You know if you needed help with your fly, all you had to do was ask me." Smiley mentions.

"Yeah, hilarious Smiley but can we do this please?" Milo says.

"So, that's Smiley." Baker whispers. "You got the stuff?" Angel asks. "Show me the money." Milo responds back.

"Fuck that." Gamble says. "Show us the stuff."

"Relax Proctor." Smiley retorts.

"That's Gamble motherfucker! I heard about you and I ain't afraid." Gamble assures.

"You have no idea how happy that makes me." Smiley replies back.

Baker looks at Tom and says, "I think I like this Smiley guy." Tom looks back at Baker and says, "He certainly has personality." Baker grabs the microphone and whispers, "Get this moving. We don't have all night."

"Yo, Smiley! Can't we do this? Angel asks. "Yeah, Smiley" Milo chimes in. "Let's get this over with." Smiley sniffs and asks, "You guys smell something?"

"Smell something? Nigga, what the fuck—" Gamble asks but is cut off by a loud gunshot.

All of the officers take out their weapons and one officer declares, "Shots fired! Shots fired." Baker moves to the center of the room with his hands out and says in a loud whisper, "Wait a minute. Just wait."

"Excuse me?" Smiley asks. "Oh shit!" Gamble yells back. "What the fuck man! You almost shot me." Baker looks at all of the officers and says, "It was just a warning shot. Everyone relax. Don't move yet. "I was speaking. You interrupt me again; the next one won't be an accident" Smiley replies.

"Chill Smiley. No need to be hostile." Milo says. "I asked if you smelled anything" Smiley repeats his question. Milo sniffs and says, "Man, I don't smell shit."

"That is exactly my point. Angel, you said you were taking a crap?" Smiley asks.

"Oh shit." Baker says.

"Uhh, yeah I was t-taking a shit. Why?" Angel says nervously.

"Well, I don't smell anything, I never heard the toilet flush, and I didn't hear you wash your hands. That's very unsanitary." Smiley says.

Baker, Tom, and the other officers look at each other very nervously. "Fuck." Baker states.

"Tell me the truth. You wearing a wire?" Smiley asks. Baker takes the mic and whispers, "You need to diffuse this situation right now. Get back on track."

Angel laughs nervously and says, "Smiley, you are buggin' the fuck out. You know that?"

"What about you Gamble?" Smiley says. "You like cheese like him? What kind of cheese do you like?"

"I ain't no fucking snitch!" Gamble yells. "Yeah, but I bet your boyfriend is though. Check him out." Smiley responds in a very smooth tone.

The officers hear footsteps march over to Angel. "Let's settle this shit. This motherfucker ain't wearing-"
Gamble stops speaking as the police hear the loud rustling of clothes. There is a banging on the mic that Angel is wearing. The sound is so loud, the technician has to take his headphones off. All of the officers now start to get out of their seats.

"Yo, what the fuck is this shit?" Gamble yells.

Baker slowly stands up and says, "Everyone stand by."

"How about that? I bet the cops are standing by." Smiley exclaims. The officers can hear Gamble breathing very heavy. Baker grabs the mic and starts to say something, but he's not sure what to say.

"You bitch ass nigga!!" Gamble yells. "You a snitch. Huh, motherfucker?"

"Gamble, no! Wait! Please!!" Angel pleads.

Tom looks at Baker and says, "You have to move in now before it's too—"

There are several loud gunshots.

All of the officers run out of the apartment, down the stairs and out of the building. They all run across the street with their guns drawn and into the other building. Tom starts to run in the building as well when Baker stops him right before he enters.

"No Tom, you wait here." Baker says with his hand on Tom's shoulder. Tom pushes his hand off and yells, "Are you fucking crazy! You need all the help you can get."

"But this is not your op, and you're just an observer." Baker remarks back. "If anything happened to you on my op, it would be my ass. Just stay here. If anyone makes it past us or if you see anything, let us know right away."

Baker runs in the building, and Tom stands there for a minute. After a few moments, he hears a loud bang and a crash from the garbage cans in the alley. Tom looks down the alley but doesn't see anyone. He goes to the front entrance of the building and sees if any cops are coming out and none do. Tom looks down the alley again, takes a deep breath, draws his service weapon and slowly walks down the alley. He comes to a pile of trash bags and sees Smiley laying there motionless trying to camouflage himself. Smiley is in his late forties with salt and pepper hair but has an otherwise pleasant looking face. Smiley also has blood on his face and clothes. He is wearing a pair of dress pants and a long sleeve button down shirt. Tom grabs him by the jacket, and they wrestle on the ground, but Smiley is too weak to fight back. Tom stands Smiley up and throws him against the wall and slaps a pair of handcuffs on him.

"You're under arrest asshole." Tom says.

"No. Wait." Smiley says in a weak voice.

"You have the right to remain silent." Tom says as he is reading Smiley his rights.

"Five thousand." Smiley mumbles. "What?" Tom says shocked. "I'll give you five thousand dollars to get me to a doctor." Smiley says slightly louder.

"Bribing an officer? Are you fucking kidding me?" Tom says as he walks Smiley out of the alley.

"Ten thousand." Smiley continues.

"You're just digging yourself in a deeper hole. Keep talking." Tom says.

"Fifteen thousand." Smiley says. Tom stops walking and asks, "You'll give me fifteen thousand dollars if I get you to a doctor?"

"Yes." Smiley replies nodding his head.

Tom moves closer to Smiley and whispers, "Do you have twenty thousand dollars?"

Smiley smiles slightly and says, "I can get it."

"Don't you fucking smile at me. I mean right now?" Tom asks. "Right now." Smiley replies.

Tom turns Smiley so they can face each other. Tom looks him square in the eye and says, "You're not fucking with me, right?"

Smiley says, "Look at me. I've been shot, and I'm losing a lot of blood. I can't afford to fuck around. You get me to a doctor, and I will get you twenty thousand dollars."

Tom looks at Smiley up and down. He then looks down the alleyway and says, "Let's go."

*

Sometime later, Baker and the other officers are coming out of the building. Some are shaking their heads in disbelief. Additional officers arrive in squad cars soon followed vehicles from the New York City Fire Department and Emergency Services Department. The last vehicle to approach the scene is one from the City Medical Examiner's Office. The street is closed off in both directions, and there is now a helicopter flying overhead. Tom, now in his car is slowly driving up the road. He approaches the blockade and signals for Baker to come over.

"You're leaving?" Baker asks.

Yeah. Amy called again. I have to find out what's going on at home." Tom answers back.

"What is going on at home? You guys OK?" Baker asks. Tom just stares at him saying nothing then slowly looks away. Baker looks at Tom and says, "I'm sorry. That's none of my business."

"What happened here?" Tom asks looking behind him.

Baker turns around to face the building and says, "Everyone's dead. Everyone except Smiley. We think he got out. He's the only one not accounted for. We did a door by door search of the entire floor but so far, no luck. We think he might have jumped out the window and ran down the street." Baker turns back to Tom and asks, "You didn't see anyone run past you right, Tom?"

"No one came through here." Tom says.

"That's what I figured. If someone did, they would be no match for the NYPD's most decorated officer. He would have handled it." Baker says with a big smile. Tom smiles back very weakly. "He's gotta be around here somewhere. We'll find him." Baker says. Baker extends his hand and says, "Listen, Tom it was good seeing you and congrats on the award." Tom shakes his hand and says, "Likewise. Thanks for letting me tag along. Let me know when you find him."

"Sure thing." Baker says. He turns down the street and yells at an officer sitting in his squad car. "Hey! Move your car! An officer is trying to get by." The officer moves his car enough for Tom to get by. The officer and Tom wave to each other and Tom drives down the street.

Tom drives for a good while until the helicopter and the police lights are a reasonable distance away. He then slowly pulls over and says, "Hey. You still alive back there? Don't die on me!"

"I'm still here. Just go to the address I gave you." Smiley says in a faint voice. Tom starts slowly driving again.

*

They are now in an apartment which looks like a makeshift clinic. There are several lounge chairs in the living room. Each chair has an adjoining IV pole. Smiley is sitting at one of those chairs which is attached to an IV while the doctor treats his gunshot wound. The doctor is a man in his sixties with a balding head and horn-rimmed glasses.

Tom looks around the room and asks the doctor, "What hospital are you affiliated with?"

Smiley and the doctor look at each other then Smiley then bursts out into laughter. He laughs so hard; tears fall from his eyes. He smiles at Tom and says, "The doctor is what you call an independent consultant for the underbelly of the Bronx. You see, he lost his medical license years ago after getting caught up in a scam."

"Which is all bullshit if you ask me!" The doctor yells.

"What was the name of the cop who put you away?" Smiley asks.

"That asshole didn't put me away. He's not a cop." The doctor says back defensively.

"No. But he did shut down your entire operation singlehandedly. Come on, what was his name?" Smiley asks again.

The doctor looks at Smiley and says, "His name was Dhack Winston, but most people knew him as The Mad Hatter.

Smiley snaps his fingers and says, "That's it! Hey, why do they call him the Mad Hatter?" The doctor rolls his eyes and says, "I never asked."

He takes out a business card and hands it to Tom. Tom hesitates at first then slowly takes the card. The doctor says, "I make house calls."

"He has the best hands in the business." Smiley says.

The doctor accidentally hurts Smiley while stitching him up. Smiley winces in pain and asks, "Fuck! Is this your first day?" Smiley smiles through what the doctor is doing.

The doctor says, "Why don't you let me give you something for the pain? How can you smile through this?"

Smiley looks at the doctor and says, "Physical pain is more manageable than psychological distress. This pain will eventually go away. But the pain from mental abuse will last forever."
"You speak from experience?" The doctor asks. Smiley turns to the doctor and says, "We all do."

There is a loud knock on the door. The doctor looks at Tom and asks, "Can you get that?" Tom slowly gets up as the banging on the door gets louder. Tom opens the door, and Boozer pushes past him. He is an overweight black man in his mid-forties although he looks a lot older than that. He wheezes a lot. Behind him is Percival, who is a tall, muscular black man in his late teens. Coming in last is Woody. He is a young and very unassuming black man in his early thirties.

Boozer and Smiley slap hands. "Smiley." Boozer says. Smiley looks at Boozer up and down and says, "You look terrible."

Boozer deeply signs and says, "I know. I know. I need my meds." He turns to the doctor and yells, "Doc, you brought my shit?"

The doctor reaches into his bag, pulls out a bottle of pills and tosses them to Boozer. He immediately opens the bottle and takes two of them. "It would probably be best if you lost about seventy or eighty pounds." The doctor pleads while looking at him.

"I know. I know. It's bad enough you told me to give up drinking. I have to stop fucking eating too?" Boozer asks. He tosses the doctor a roll of money held together by rubber bands. The doctor catches it with one hand and stuffs it in his shirt pocket.

"You also need to reduce the stress in your life. If your heart works too hard, you'll have a massive coronary and be dead before you hit the floor." The doctor mentions.

"But I can still fuck, right?" Boozer asks with an awkward smile on his face.

"Yes. But no marathon nights. Those days are over." The doctor says.

Smiley looks at Boozer and says, "That's fine. He only needs two minutes."

"Hey, fuck you!" Boozer says to Smiley and they both laugh.

Woody looks at Smiley and asks, "You OK?" "I got shot. I've been shot before, and I'll probably get shot again." Smiley replies.

Percival stands up and marches over to Smiley. He almost pushes Boozer out of the way. He gets right in Smiley's face and yells, "What the fuck happened?"

Smiley smiles at him and says, "Percival! Percy! When did you get out of jail?" Percival stands very close to Smiley and says, "You think I'm fucking playing games with you? You tell me what happened or I'll beat the fucking shit outta you!" Smiley just smiles at him and says nothing. "You think I'm afraid of you? I heard all about you. I ain't fucking scared of you." Percival yells.

Smiley, who is still smiling, starts to stand up when Boozer stands in between them slowly. Boozer looks at Percival and says, "Calm the fuck down. Go stand over there before you do something you'll regret later." Percival stares at Boozer for a minute then slowly walks away to the other side of the room.

Boozer sits in the lounge chair next to Smiley and asks, "What happened?"

Smiley looks around the room and says, "Gamble found out Angel was a snitch and was wearing a wire, so he started shooting up the place." Percival points to Tom and asks, "And who the fuck is this?"

Smiley looks at Tom and says, "He's the cop that got me out. We owe him twenty grand by the way." Boozer looks at Smiley with his mouth open. "What?" Boozer asks in disbelief.

"A deal's a deal." Smiley says.

Percival grabs Smiley's bag and sits back down. He opens the bag and takes out an expensive looking camera and slams it on the floor. "Take it easy with that! That camera costs more than your whole outfit." Smiley barks. Percival looks Smiley in the face and says, "You don't know what the fuck you're talking about."

Smiley looks Percival up and down. He adjusts himself in his seat, smiles and says, "You just got here. I don't know where Ridley found you, but you're not very high up on the totem pole so I know you don't get paid that much. But you still want to look like you're hot shit so, between the pants, shirt, shoes, socks, and underwear, your entire outfit has to cost about two hundred and seventy-five dollars. I'm pretty sure some of that money was borrowed so you can look the part. The lens on that camera is nine hundred dollars. The camera itself is another seven hundred fifty. The total cost of the piece of equipment in your hand is one thousand six hundred and fifty dollars. The difference between this camera is your outfit is thirteen hundred seventy-five dollars. That's where you are on the food chain." Percival looks around the room, and Tom stares at him. The doctor shrugs his shoulders. Woody is trying to hide his smirk, but Boozer is smiling widely and snickers at him and says, "He's probably right, you know."

Percival drops the camera on the floor, stands up and says, "You know what? I fucking tired of your shit!" He marches over to Smiley with both fists clenched. As soon as he takes two steps, Smiley takes out a gun from his waistband and shoots Percival in the leg. He screams in pain and falls to the floor holding his leg. Everyone in the apartment tenses up. As soon as he hits the ground, the doctor stands up and starts to make his way toward Percival.

Smiley grabs the doctor's arm and asks, "Where are you going?"

The doctor looks at Smiley and says, "He's been shot. I need to take a look at him."

"No, you don't. You're not done with me yet. Let him sit there for a while and bleed. Sit down." Smiley says. The doctor looks over at Percival again then at Smiley and slowly sits down and continues to treat him. Smiley then looks at Percival and asks, "What's the matter? Nothing to say? I thought you were tough. Give me some of that he-man nigger talk. You know what I'm talking about." Smiley clears his throat and says in his pseudo fake thug-like voice, "Ayo, you gonna let dat nigga do you like dat? Handle yo bizness son. Yeah, fuck dat shit." Smiley's smile slowly fades away as he says in his normal voice, "Now get up, come over here and teach me a lesson. But as soon as you get up, I will put you back down, and you will never get up again." Smiley aims his gun at Percival in the traditional way and says, "You want me to shoot you like this?" He then aims the gun at Percival sideways and says, "I know most people like you like to hold the gun this way because it makes you look cool. This is the worst way to hold a gun because it causes the gun to jam." Smiley then aims the gun at him upside down and says, "How about this way? Or does it matter how I aim the gun at you? You want to play catch? I throw a bullet and you catch it." Smiley cocks the gun, aims it at Percival the traditional way and slightly smiles. Percival's lip starts to quiver as Boozer stands in between him and Percival.

Smiley smiles at Boozer and says, "What are you doing? Move over." Boozer turns to Percival and says, "What did I say? You don't fucking listen. I told you not to fuck with Smiley. He don't hesitate."

Smiley looks at Percival, sees the fear in his eyes and says, "When the doctor is finished with me, he'll take a look at you." He then turns to Boozer and says, "Pay this guy so he can go." Boozer takes money out of Smiley's backpack. Tom stands up waiting for his money.

Boozer looks at Tom and says, "Give me your number."

"Why?" Tom asks. "Because it's always good to have another cop on the payroll." Boozer says. They put his money in a plastic bag and hands it to Tom. He slowly walks over to Boozer and gives him his number and takes the bag. "You can go now." Boozer says to Tom.

Tom walks over to the front door. Boozer unlocks and opens the door. As he starts to walk out, Smiley says, "Thanks for before. I appreciate it." Tom turns around and says, "I hope I never see you again." Tom leaves.

Outside the apartment, Tom is breathing very heavy. He looks at the money in the bag and rolls his eyes. He hears giggling inside. Tom walks down the stairs.

Inside the apartment, Boozer says out loud, "Someone should follow him. Find out where he lives." Woody says, "I'll do it."

Boozer looks at Smiley and says, "Seriously, who the fuck was that?"

Smiley looks at Boozer and says, "I'm not sure. But he was very desperate for the money to get me out of there."

*

Back at his house, Amy is sitting in the kitchen surrounded by the papers from earlier. The ashtray is filled with cigarette butts. Tom walks in and sees Amy running her fingers through her hair. He sees the butts in the ashtray and says, "I thought you quit."

Amy stands up and bellows, "Look who decided to fucking come home to reality. I'm sitting here wondering what the best next move for us is and stressed beyond belief. So yeah, I started smoking again. Do you have any idea what we should do? Any clues? Probably not, right?"

"I have one." Tom says rather smugly. Tom takes the plastic bag, holds it upside down and dumps all of the money in front of her. Amy sits there in stunned silence with her mouth open. She looks at him and smiles slightly. She picks up a stack of money and fans through it. Looking at the money, she asks, "How much is here?"

"Twenty thousand." Tom says. Amy looks up sharply at him. She then looks down at the money and takes another random stack of cash and fans through it.

Tom leans forward and asks, "Aren't you going to ask me where I got it? How I got it? What I had to do to get it?"

After a few seconds of looking down at the money, Amy looks up and says, "It's not my place to ask your business. It's my place to support my man as he works hard to provide for his family." She gathers all of the money on the table and pulls it closer to her and says. "I'll take this money and make sure everything in the house is taken care of. That's my place." Amy takes the money and gently puts it back in the bag. As soon as she does, Sabrina comes halfway down the stairs with her music blasting on her phone.

She takes the headphones off and asks, "Mom, what are you shouting about? What's going on?" She sees her father standing next to the table, and she rolls her eyes saying, "Oh, it's only you. When are you going to teach me how to drive?"

"Don't talk to your father like that! After all the sacrifices he's made for us." Amy snaps.

Sabrina comes down the stairs and snarks, "What sacrifices? He hasn't done anything for us in years."

Amy stands up, walks over to Sabrina, gets right in her face and says in a booming loud voice, "And I said don't fucking talk to your father like that. He does work hard for both of us, so show him a little fucking respect, you ingrate!" Sabrina looks at her mother and her face falls. She looks at Tom who has no expression at all. She slowly turns around and walks back upstairs.

Amy turns to Tom and says in a sweet voice, "I know you had a hard but productive day today. You must be starving. Want me to fix you something to eat?"

Tom looks at the stairs where his daughter went then looks at Amy. He slowly shakes his head and walks upstairs.

Chapter Three

Woody and Boozer are in a car going down Bronxwood Ave. Woody is driving, and Boozer is on the passenger side. Boozer is looking at a piece of paper. He turns to Woody and says, "Slow down. I think it's close." Woody slows the car down until they come to Tom's house on the corner. They stop at the stop sign and look at Tom's house. They see several day laborers working on the roof.

Woody turns to Boozer and says, "Look at how many people are on the roof. What do you think that means?" Boozer looks at the house and says, "It means this is how he chooses to spend his money." Boozer takes out his phone and takes a few pictures of the workers on the rooftop. The car behind them honks their horn. Woody puts the car in drive and moves it slowly away from the house.

"Where to now?" Woody asks.

Boozer turns to him and says, "Take me to Joanna's."

*

Woody stops in front of JEM's laundromat. Boozer gets out, and Woody drives away. Boozer walks inside to find a few people doing their laundry. A man with an outraged look on his face walks over to Joanna who is sitting behind the counter towards the back of the establishment. She is an Asian woman of about sixty-five years old but could pass for a woman at least ten years younger. Joanna has auburn hair, but her roots are growing in which are a combination of both grey and white. She is wearing red reading glasses that are attached to a cord around her neck and walks with a slight limp. Joanna is reading a Chinese language magazine. The man walks over to her and yells, "The dyer has broken again!"

She takes off her glasses and lets them hang down her neck. She slowly looks up to the man and asks, "What you say? What no work?"

"The dryer doesn't work." The man says again. He points to the dryer in question. She looks behind him at the dryer. Joanna turns to him confused and says, "It work. What you mean it no work. It work! Look!" She points to the dryer. The man shakes his head and says, "I know it works but—"

"But you just say it no work. It work!" Joanna says loudly.

The man moves closer to her and says, "I just put a quarter in, and it didn't give me more time." Joanna looks at him and says, "Wha?!?"

"Time! More time?" The man yells at her. Joanna looks at her watch and says, "It almost four clock."

"What the fuck are you talking about?" The man yells. "You ask me for time. I give you time!" Joanna says back slamming her magazine.

She glances over at Boozer and catches him smiling. She frowns slightly at him and goes back to the customer. Boozer has to cover his face and turn away to prevent the man from seeing him laugh.

"How the fuck can you run a business if you can't even understand English!" The man yells.

Joanna now stands up and looks the man in the face. "No yell at me! I old woman! I work hard! You say machine no work! Machine work! See! You no yell at me! I no yell at you! You ask for time! I give you time! I give you time!"

"Just forget it. It's only a quarter." The man walks away. Joanna's daughter Emily comes upstairs from the basement. She is a pretty young woman of about nineteen years old. She has straight short black hair.

Boozer slowly walks towards Joanna, and she smiles slightly. "It's only a quarter?" He asks. She looks around to see if anyone is listening to them. She also looks for the man she was just talking to. She looks over Boozer's shoulder and sees him talking on the phone in a very animated manner. She then leans forward to Boozer and says without the exaggerated accent, "A quarter here. A quarter there. By the end of the week, I have an extra fifteen dollars in profit."

Boozer looks up at her with a fake shocked face. He gasps and says, "Why Miss Joanna, whatever happened to your accent?"

"You know how many people I know, immigrants I mean that pretend not to understand English but know exactly what the fuck is going on around them? These people think we're stupid? They're the dumb ones. Meanwhile, he cheats on his wife and his girlfriend. He drinks too much and thinks too little." Joanna says. She takes his hand and says, "Enough of that. You want to go downstairs?" "That's why I'm here." Boozer responds. They both look at Emily. She looks at both of them and says, "Try not to make a mess. I just cleaned up down there."

Joanna takes a very steep staircase downstairs to the cellar. Boozer followers her down. He takes a look around the room.

There are many rice bags all over the floor. There are also shelves on the walls with detergent and fabric softener. Boozer takes a quick look around and says, "This place is clean." Joanna walks over to him and holds him. "Do you remember the first time we met?" she asks.

"Of course." Boozer responds back. "You were running that quarter scam on a customer, he got angry, slapped you around and threatened to have you deported."

"So, you threw him out a window." Joanna says. "I knew you were a dealer." "And I knew you spoke perfect English and ran scams on customers." Boozer replies to her.

"And when the cops came, we covered each other." Joanna says.

"They were really hard on you. Because years ago, you ran with the Triads." Boozer says. They look at each other. Joanna walks away from him slightly and says, "We've had this conversation before. That was a lifetime ago. Way before Emily was born. I started as a translator, and then I was a courier."

"I read in the paper from years ago; you were about to make a drop on a house when the feds came in and arrested everyone inside." Boozer says looking very puzzled. Joanna smiles slightly. "The feds claimed they got a reliable tip and acted on it." Boozer continues. "Look at you looking through the archives! The feds came after me, and I ran as fast and as far as I could." Joanna says. "I don't think I ever –"
"And how much were you carrying?" Boozer says interrupting her. "I read somewhere between one and two million. Is that true?" He continues.

Joanna smiles and says, "You read more than I can remember. I think so." "But they never found the money." Boozer says.

"Never. I dropped it. I can't even remember where. I went to jail for ten years, and that was that. Everyone I dealt with was sent to prison, sent back to China or killed." Joanna says. "And your crazy cousin owns this place?" Boozer asks. "This and the Chinese restaurant." Joanna responds back.

Boozer looks around the room and asks, "Do you ever miss it? The life?" Joanna takes a long look at him and says, "Those days were good. Some of those days were even great. But those days are gone and they are never coming back. Look, not for nothing but are we gonna fuck or not?" Joanna starts to take her pants off. Boozer does the same. Joanna leans over a small folding table and says, "You have to be quiet. I have customers upstairs."

"Relax. I can do that." Boozer responds. "You also have to go slow. I don't want you to have a stroke or something." Joanna continues.

"Not a problem." Boozer explains. "The doctor gave me my pills."

Upstairs, Emily is sitting behind the counter when Smiley walks in. He is wearing a pair of dress pants and a long sleeve button down shirt. "Smiley." Emily says in a very professional manner. "Emily." Smiley says back the same way.

"Where's big man?" He asks.

Emily lets out a huge sigh and says, "Downstairs with my mom." Smiley starts to go down there, and she says, "You might want to give them a few minutes." Smiley stands there and stares at Emily for about ten seconds then says, "That should be enough time."

He goes downstairs and sees Boozer wheezing very hard and sitting down. Joanna is still naked from the waist down holding his face. "That was fast." Smiley says with a slight smile.

"Hand….me….my…… pills." Boozer says. Joanna grabs his pills, opens them up, takes one out and hands it to him. Boozer pops the fill in his mouth. Smiley looks at Boozer's sweaty face and says, "Maybe you should take another pill." Joanna looks at his face and says, "Maybe you should get out of this life. This business isn't for you anymore."

Boozer sits up, looks her square in the eye and says, "And how do I do that? Just walk in and hand in my resignation? You don't get out of this life. Not ever. And even if I could, what then? What kind of job could I possibly get? 'What kind of skills do you have Mr. Boozer. Well, I've been in the drug trade for a very long time. I deal with people pretty well, and I take short lunch breaks.' Are you for real? At this stage and this age, there's no way out of this life. And the life will catch up to you. One way or the other." He takes a long look at Smiley and says, "You've been doing this shit longer than me. You don't get stressed out by this life? How?"

Smiley looks at Boozer, smiles slightly and says, "I sleep with the lights out." Boozer snarls at him and says, "Well I can't do that." "Maybe I can put on a night light for you." Smiley responds back.

"Fuck you. I know you keep thinking about starting your little project. You need to give up that pipe dream. Where will you even go to start that up? You really think you can just walk away from this life?" Boozer asks.

Smiley drops his smile and looks intently at Boozer and says, "All I need is the opportunity. And when it presents itself, I will not hesitate to take advantage of it."

Joanna's phone rings. She answers it saying, "Hello. Hey Lee. How are you? No. Everything is fine. I was just an accident. Yes. He pushed me to the ground, but other people stepped in. No need for you to come down. NO! I don't need your stupid trigger-happy ass down here. You hear me? Good-bye!" She hangs up, looks at Boozer and Smiley and says, "He will kill someone one day."

"You think your cousin can hook me up with a discount on some pork fried rice?" Boozer asks. "You know you really shouldn't be eating that food." Joanna says.

"Anyway, you called me? What do you want?" Smiley asks. Boozer looks at Joanna who takes the hint and goes up the stairs. As soon as she is out of sight, Boozer says, "Ridley is pissed you gave that cop twenty grand." "I had no choice. What was I supposed to do? I was shot and losing blood. If I'd gone to a hospital, I would have been arrested. And don't think for one minute I wouldn't have cut a deal to save my own ass. I'm not going to do thirty years while you idiots enjoy life on the outside. You think I'm going to take one for the team?" Smiley says.

"Well, it's not like you haven't done that before." Boozer says.

Smiley smiles at Boozer and says, "Go fuck your mother." They both laugh. "There's something else." Boozer says very concerned. "What happened, now?" Smiley replies.

"I think they know you've been skimming off the top for years." Boozer says. "You mean we've been skimming off the top for years." Smiley responds right back.

"Over the years, we've cut so many corners, you could probably build a wall." Smiley says. "Where's your wall?" Boozer asks. Smiley stares at him for a second then says, "Where's yours?" They look at each other for a few seconds then Smiley finally says, "He really must have needed that money. He seems almost desperate." "Well, when Woody and me drove past there, he was fixing up his house." Boozer says.

"Where does he live?" Smiley asks.

"Astor and Bronxwood Avenues. This whole thing has created an interesting situation and a little problem." Boozer says. Smiley looks at Boozer and says, "What do you mean? What kind of problem?

Chapter Four

Tom is walking down the sidewalk and looks at numbers in front of a tenement building. He checks the text message from his phone. Tom walks inside and steps in the elevator. He gets off at his floor and walks down the hallway looking at numbers on the door. He refers again to the text message and finds the door he is looking for. Tom is about to knock when he sees a mother and child walk past. He nervously and politely smiles until they pass. After they pass by him and are out of sight, he looks at the door for a while, takes and deep breath and knocks.

The door opens just enough for a double barrel shotgun to be pointed at him. The man holding the shotgun is named Lando. He is a young, thin black man. "Hands up, rookie." He snarls as he leans forward and grabs Tom to bring him in the house. Tom puts his hands up slightly.

"Close the door and lock it." Lando says with the gun still pointed at Tom's head. Tom lowers his hands slightly and says, "Look, there's no—"

"I said close and lock the fucking door!!" Lando yells. He presses the shotgun against Tom's forehead. "OK. OK. Relax." Tom says as he closes the door and locks it. Lando pushes Tom up against the door and says, "Up against the wall." Tom puts both hands on the front door with his legs spread. Lando has one hand with the gun aimed at his head and roughly frisks him with the other hand. "You don't have to do that so rough, you know?" Tom pleads. Lando stops what he's doing and gets way in Tom's face and snarls, "Now you know how it feels." He continues to pat Tom down until he finds his service pistol. Lando takes it away and turns Tom around.

"You can't take that." Tom says almost defiantly.

Lando motions Tom to go to the kitchen and says, "This way rookie."

Lando leads Tom to the kitchen where Big Ben and Ridley are waiting. Big Ben is a very overweight black man. He's in his mid-forties with a giant afro. He is sitting at the kitchen table eating Chinese food. Next to him is Ridley who is a very intimidating looking black man in his mid to late forties. Tom takes a look around the kitchen and sees drugs, money, and guns strewn all over the place.

"You can put your hands down now officer." Ridley says in his deep baritone voice.

Tom puts his hands down and asks, "What the hell is all this? Did you call me?" "I did." Ridley responds. "I wanted to meet the man who took my twenty thousand dollars."

Tom looks nervously at Ridley, Big Ben, and Lando and says, "First of all, I didn't take it. That Smiley guy offered it to me to get him out. If you have a problem with any of this, take it up with him." Ridley leans back in his chair and says, "I'm not blaming Smiley. He did what he had to do to get out. But that money had a purpose. A very particular purpose."

"Are you Clayton?" Tom asks.

Ridley chuckles a little and says, "No. I ain't Clayton, man."

"Who are you then?" Tom asks.

Lando gets way in Tom's face and barks, "Never mind who the fuck he is." Ridley stands up and circles Tom looking at him up and down. He smiles slightly and turns to Ben and asks, "Yo, Big Ben. What you think?"

Big Ben puts down his chicken wing and grabs a paper towel to wipe his hands. He looks at Tom up and down while taking a huge gulp of his malt liquor says, "He's a pussy and totally out of his element. He has no fucking clue."

Tom takes a slight step forward and glances at Lando who is still holding the shotgun on him. He looks at Ridley and Big Ben and says, "I'm no pussy."

"You took the money fast enough but never thought about the consequences. There are always consequences. About twenty thousand of them." Big Ben says.

Ridley stands again, and Tom tenses up a little as he measures Ridley's imposing size and height. Ridley says to him, "To answer your question, I work very closely with Clayton. And I have a problem."

"What does that have to do with me." Tom asks. "You're gonna help me solve it. You see, I needed that money too." Ridley responds to Tom. Ridley then looks at Lando and motions with his head. Lando nods knowingly. He looks at Tom, then lowers his gun and leaves the kitchen. Big Ben slowly stands up and moves his hand closer to a weapon on the table. While he's gone, Ridley and Big Ben look intensely at Tom. Tom looks at both of them and turns his eyes to the floor.

"OK." Lando yells from another room. Ridley and Big Ben both stand up. Ridley grabs a huge gun and says, "This way."

"Where are we going?" Tom asks. Ridley looks around the kitchen and replies, "We can't do this shit in here. It's unsanitary."

"Do what?" Tom asks very nervously. Ridley walks out of the kitchen, but Tom just stands there. Big Ben taps him on the shoulder with a gun and motions for Tom to follow Ridley. Tom walks out with Big Ben close behind.

All three go to a back bedroom where Lando is standing over someone. This person has their hands tied behind their back and wearing a hood over their head. The hood is covered in blood and is dripping down their shirt.
"Who's that?" Tom asks in a very nervous voice.

"That money was for, among other things, to kill this motherfucker." Ridley says. Tom looks at everyone in the room and asks, "Kill him for what?"

Ridley moves closer to the person and says, "He's a rat bitch nigga who only looks out for themselves."

"Ridley, I swear. I would never—" The person says.

Lando smacks this person upside the head with a gun causing a scream. "Shut the fuck up!" He screams in his face. Ridley looks at Big Ben and nods. Big Ben walks Tom over to the closet and opens it. Tom looks inside and sees no clothes. He looks up on the shelf and sees a gun lying there. He turns to Ridley who says, "Our problem is now your problem."

Tom looks at the gun in the closet, then looks at looks at Ridley and asks, "You think I'm gonna kill him?" "I know you will." Ridley responds. "When you took money from us, you crossed the line. There's no going back."

"Go fuck yourself." Tom says defiantly.

"Maybe I should call in a tip on how Smiley really got out of that building." Ridley says. Tom looks at Ridley up and down and says, "They won't fucking believe you."

Ridley walks over to Tom and asks, "How's that work on your house going?" Tom gasps slightly, and his eyes get wide. "Getting your roof fixed, huh?" Ridley continues.

"You've been to my fucking house?" Tom asks. Big Ben hands Ridley his phone. Ridley starts swiping through the pictures Big Ben took.

"You have at least five Mexicans working on your roof. Woody said he saw a plumber's van outside your house the other day and I know they're expensive as fuck! Those Mexicans are most likely illegal, so they can only take cash. How the fuck can you explain how you got all that cash so fast? You went to the bank and got a fucking loan? They'll check it all out and put two and two together." Ridley explains.

Tom's eyes get very wide, and he starts to breathe very rapidly. Big Ben starts laughing loudly and says, "Look at this white boy. He can't fuck with us. Him against us? What!?!"

"You already took the money. I'm making this easy. All you have to do is pull the trigger and walk away. If not, you'll have a lot more to lose than we will. I promise you that." Ridley says. "Please man, I'm begging you. Don't do this." the person says.

Ridley takes off the hood, and the person is Beck. Ridley starts punching Beck in the face who screams in pain. Ridley looks at

Tom then looks at the gun in the closet. Tom begins to reach for the gun but hesitates. Ridley says, "Relax officer. This gun has a purpose, and we've done this kind of thing before. We have bigger fish to fry, and it doesn't include you."

Tom walks toward the closet and grabs the gun. He turns to Beck and moves closer to him. Now standing over him, Tom slowly points the weapon at Beck's chest. "Please don't." Becks pleads before Tom shoots him. Becks falls over dead. Ridley now walks over to Tom and says, "Shoot him again. This time in the head to be sure." Tom talks over to Beck's body and shoots him point blank in the head. Tom drops the gun.

Ridley looks at him, smiles slightly and says, "Good boy."

Big Ben stands over Beck's body and says, "I'll take care of the body. I know exactly what to do."

Ridley turns to Big Ben and says, "Clayton called me. He has plans for this one." Ridley looks at Tom and says, "You can go now officer. I'll call you again when I need you."

Lando holds Tom by the arm and leads him out of the apartment. He hands Tom back his service weapon, unlocks the door, opens it and ushers Tom out. Tom leaves and hears Lando lock the door from the inside. "Where did Smiley find this motherfucker?" Tom hears Ridley say through the door. He then hears Lando, Ridley and Big Ben giggling from the inside of the apartment. Tom starts to go down the stairs. He stops midway and starts breathing very heavily. He sits on the stairs and continues to breathe heavy. After a few moments, Tom slowly stands up. He starts to walk down the stairs when his phone goes off. He looks at it and says, "Oh shit." He walks a little faster down the stairs.

Tom and Amy are in the car driving down a street with very nice homes on either side. Amy is dressed in very fancy clothes while Tom is dressed more plainly.

"I hope we're not late." Amy says. "I said I'm sorry. I got held up. I had a rough day." Tom replies back. While driving, Tom glances at what Amy is wearing. "You got all dressed up for this?" Amy looks at herself, fixes her hair and says, "Well, I like to look the part." She looks at him up and down and says, "You could have tried harder."

"Didn't I just tell you I had a rough day today?! Please don't start with me. I don't need this shit today." Tom barks.

"Fine. I won't start." Amy says. "But you know how important this is to me. Try not to embarrass me." She continues.

"I'll do my best." Tom dryly replies. She points to a huge Victorian style house and says, "That must be the house. Oh, and there's Darren." They pull over and get out of the car. Amy walk over to Darren with her hand extended. Darren is a young white male. He shakes her hand with a huge smile and asks, "Amy Sims?"

"That's me! You must be Darren." Amy replies with a huge smile. "Darren Robertson. A pleasure." Darren says.

"The pleasure is all mine. This is my husband Tom." Amy says and ushers Tom to move closer to Darren who extends his hand out to Tom with a smile and says, "How are you Tom?" He glances over at Amy and forces a slight smile and says, "I'm fine."

"Amy tells me you're a New York City Police Officer. How long have been on the job?" Tom asks.

Tom takes a deep breath and says, "Almost twenty-four years." "Wow! That's a long time." Darren says very enthusiastically. Amy moves closer to Tom and puts her arm around him and says, "He's finally going to be retiring soon. We're thinking about the next stage in our lives."

"Which is why you're here. Come! Let's take a look at the house." Darren leads them to the inside of the house.

He opens the door to a vast foyer area with a big chandelier hanging overhead. Directly ahead of them is a staircase that leads to the upstairs. Amy looks around with her eyes widened and mouth opened. "Wow! Look at this place! It's beautiful!"

"What's the square footage of this house?" Tom asks. Darren looks at his paper and reads, "This house is twenty-seven hundred square feet with four bedrooms, two full bathrooms, an attic, finished basement, three car garage and a huge backyard that can be used for entertaining or you can put in a pool if you wish."

"Can we see the kitchen?" Amy asks. "Of course. Right, this way." Darren says. He leads them to the large and very well-lit kitchen. "This was just redone and has all new appliances and countertops. The whole house is move in ready." Darren continues.

Amy moves a little closer to Darren and asks, "What's the neighborhood like? Like what kind of people are living here currently?" Tom rolls his eyes at her. Darren frowns a little and says, "What do you mean? Everyone in this area is decent, kind and hardworking."

"Yeah, that's not really what I mean." Amy says in a low voice and looking away slightly. Darren glances at Tom who refuses to look Darren in the eye. Darren moves a little closer to Amy and says, "I'm sorry, but I don't understand the question." Amy starts to open her mouth, but Tom moves closer to Darren and says, "She wants to know if there are any Blacks, Hispanics or Albanians in the area." Darren stares at Tom and then Amy who now has a little trouble looking Darren back in the eye.

"Well…..the neighborhood does have a black mailman." Darren says. "Umm….does he lives in this area?" Amy asks rather sheepishly. Darren leans over to Amy and says in a low voice, "No. He wishes he could." He and Amy laugh a little as Tom shakes his head. "This area is rather exclusive, and the residents would like to keep it that way." Darren says softly.

"How much is this house?" Tom asks. "Nine fifty." Darren says back. "Go to hell." Tom blurts out without skipping a beat. Darren smiles a little and says, "The house is a bit pricey, but you get what you pay for. You get a house that is move in ready, close to the shops and restaurants. It's only a five-minute drive to the train station and a forty-minute ride to the city."

Amy moves closer to Tom and says, "This would be a lovely house for us. The right kind of neighborhood with the right kind of people." Tom stares straight ahead and says, "You mean the white kind of people." Amy shoots him a dirty look. Darren gives Tom his card and says with a bright smile and laughs slightly, "You know the old saying, 'Happy wife, happy life'." Tom turns to Darren and with no facial expression says, "I know another old saying, 'Pricey house, pricey spouse'." The smile on Darren's face slowly fades away.

There is a knock on the door. Darren, Tom, and Amy walk over to the door to see Debbie standing there. She is a middle-aged woman with dark hair. She is wearing high priced clothes and jewelry. Amy sees Debbie and walks over to her, and they embrace. "You look great!" Amy says.

"You too!" Debbie responds back. "What do you think of the house?"

Russell rushes in the house and yells, "Sold! They'll take it!" He moves over to shake Tom's hand. They shake hands and hug. "Not yet. We have a lot to talk about." Tom replies back.

Darren's face lights up and says, "So you will think about it?" Amy moves closer to Darren and says, "Yes. We certainly will."

"Fantastic! Please call me if you have any questions." Darren says. They all go outside as Darren closes the door to the house. He waves goodbye, gets in his car and leaves. Amy walks toward Debbie and says, "How far are you from here?" Both Debbie and Russell laugh and Debbie says, "We'd be practically neighbors."

Russell stands close to Debbie holding her hand and says, "I don't know about you guys but I'm starving. Can we talk more over food?"

*

They all walk in a very fancy restaurant. There are several groups of people standing in front of them. The place is full to capacity with only one table vacant. Every single person dining at this establishment is white. Amy looks around, and her face lights up. She smiles brightly and says, "I can get used to this." Tom looks at the people in front of them and the single table available. "We'll never get a table. We'll be waiting forever."

Russell puts his hand on Tom's shoulder and whispers, "Trust me. I can get us a table." Russell gets the attention of the Maître D' and motions to himself, Debbie, Tom and Amy. The Maître d' smiles, nods and motions them to come forward. Russell turns to everyone and says, "Told you I would handle it. I've had it all arranged."

They are led to their table where water and wine are waiting for them. The owner of the restaurant, Francis walks over to Russell. Russell stands up and shakes his hand warmly. While slipping something in Francis' hand as they do. "How are you, Francis?" Russell asks.

"Fantastic, Russ. Just great. This is your crew?" He asks. Russell looks at his table, smiles and says, "Yup. This is my squad. Is everything set?" Francis looks back in the kitchen and says, "In a few minutes, it'll all be ready." "Great!" Russell says and sits back down. He looks at everybody at the table and says, "I hope you guys don't mind, but I took the liberty to pre-ordering everybody's food. This saves time for us so we can catch up. Is that cool?"

Amy takes a sip of her wine and says, "Very cool Russell." Amy turns to Debbie and says, "I'm so glad we have finally had a chance to get together." "Me too! I was starting to think you were avoiding me because you never called me back." Debbie responds. Amy moves a little closer to her and says, "Oh, please don't think that. We've had issues with the roof, the plumbing and the dentist for Sabrina. We need to spend more time together." The woman smiles and nods at each other. Russell leans towards Tom and says, "And by spending time they really mean spending money." Both women laugh. "Happy wife, happy life." Debbie says as she reaches for Russell's hand. They kiss, and Russell says, "Whatever it takes." Amy tries to reach for Tom's hand, but he pulls away.

Russell puts his arm around Tom and asks, "What's the matter Tommy? Everything OK?" Tom looks at Russell then at Debbie and finally at Amy and says, "I had kind of a rough day today."

"Really what happened?" Russell asks. "I'd rather not talk about it." Tom responds meekly.

"Well, when you're on the job, you can have good days and bad days. If you finish your tour and go home in one piece, that's a good day. And for me, today was a perfect day." Russell says proudly. Debbie touches his hand again and says, "That's wonderful sweetheart. What did you do today?"

Francis leads a server who is rolling a tray with four covered plates of food. Three more servers join in to place a plate in front of Amy, Tom, Russell, and Debbie. Each server has their hand on the cover ready to lift it up. They look at Francis who in turn look at Russell. He nods at Francis, and Francis nods at the servers who lift all of the plate covers at the same time. Amy smiles and applauds at their plates. "Nicely done, Francis." Russell says. "My pleasure." Francis replies before he and the servers walk away.
Russell grabs a knife and fork and says, "Dig in guys." They all start to eat. "You were about to tell us about your day?" Amy says.

Russell takes a sip of wine and says, "Well, without getting into too much detail, I had to let people know who's in charge. That reminds me, Jason called me today."

"How is he?" Debbie asks. Russell puts his knife and fork down and says, "Not good. His lungs are failing him, so he has to use an oxygen machine to breathe." Amy takes another sip of wine and asks, "Sorry, but what happened to him to again?"

Russell stares at the table for a bit breathing very deeply. Debbie grabs his hand and squeezes it. He looks at Amy and says, "A few months after he got out of prison, he and his wife were ambushed by a masked gunman. She was dropped instantly, and he was paralyzed from the waist down."

"Did Jason fight back? Did he have time to?" Amy asks while continuing to eat her food. Tom looks at her with contempt. "No. This guy was way too fast and had perfect aim. Dropping two targets with only two shots?" Russell says.

"You think it was a hit?" Tom asks.

"That's what we all think. You know, when you're a cop who cuts corners, you make a lot of enemies. Jason had his share." Russell says. Debbie squeezes his hand and says, "You just be careful."

"Does he remember anything about that night?" Tom asks.

Russell turns to Tom and says, "Yeah. You know it's very strange. Jason says the guy said if he ever came for him, he would finish what he started." "What does that even mean?" Tom asks.

"How the fuck should I know? You know how many cops and criminals were gunning for him? He asked about you." Russell says.

"Did he?" Tom responds.

"He did. He said to stop by and see him when you get the chance. It's been a while." Russell says very intently.

Tom takes a sip of his wine and says, "I wonder why now after all this time."

"He says you would know why." Russell says to Tom. They both look at each other very intently. "Besides, I think it's about time for us to run the streets together." Russell continues.

Amy smiles and says, "I think that's a great idea." Debbie smiles at Amy and says very enthusiastically, "I agree!"

"Imagine the two of us taking over the streets of the Bronx? We could do some real damage!!" Russell says in a loud voice. So loud, he notices other people in the restaurant looking at him. He mouths 'Sorry' to the patrons and looks at his table and giggles a little. He turns to Tom and sees him trying to smile, but he doesn't seem very convincing. Russell then sees Detectives Lars and Gibbons walk over to him.

"Oh shit." Russell says as the smiles leaves his face. "What is it sweetheart?" Debbie asks. Tom and Amy exchange glances at each other.

Russell looks at Gibbons and Lars and asks, "What do you guys want?"

"You're kidding right?" Gibbons says sternly.

"We actually have good news. Remember that gun you couldn't find a while back? Well, we found it." Lars says.

Russell shifts in his seat a little and says, "Uh.. that's great. Where can I pick it up?"

"Aren't you going to ask where we found it?" Lars says. Russell doesn't say anything.

"You've been on our radar for a while. Your lifestyle and your income don't exactly add up." Gibbons says. "It really started with that Roadster outside. And this place?" he says looking around "I know you have to make reservations at least six months in advance to get a table in this joint. And not only did you get a table but you pre-ordered four prime plates? That's not cheap." Gibbons continues.

Russell clears his throat and says, "Look, fellas, there's nothing wrong with—"

"You never asked us where we found your gun." Lars says a little louder this time. Most of the people around their table have stopped eating and are watching them.

Lars bends down towards Russell's ear and says, "We never told Beck and Jazz what building to go in. We were on the roof of the tallest building in the projects. We did that so we can see everything. They happened to go to the roof of the building right next to ours. We were there with surveillance equipment ready for anything. So, imagine our surprise when we saw you kill Jazz point blank. We got it all on tape." Russell is now sweating from his brow.

"We found Beck's body earlier today with the gun you lost right beside him. He was shot twice. Once in the chest and once in the head." Gibbons says to Russell.

Russell looks at Lars and says, "Look, I….I didn't kill Beck." Gibbons moves closer to Russell and says, "Oh, you didn't kill Beck, but you aren't disputing you killed Jazz, right? Russell reaches for Debbie's hand, who slowly takes it. Amy is looking very intently at Tom who avoids looking her in the eye.

"Let's go." Lars says while putting his hand on Russell's shoulder. Russell sits there and is slightly shaking in his seat. Gibbons comes around to the other side of him and says, "Either you get up on your own, or we drag your ass out and into the fucking street. Make a choice."

Lars takes out a pair of handcuffs. Gibbons looks at him and says, "No. No. No. We made a bet. I won. I get to cuff him." Lars puts his cuffs away while Gibbons takes out his handcuffs. Russell slowly stands up.

Debbie throws her napkin on the table and asks, "Do you have to cuff him in here? Can't you let him walk out of here with a little dignity?"

Lars leans over to Debbie and says, "Anyone who has to ask for dignity, doesn't deserve it."
They put the cuffs on him and lead him outside. Debbie and Tom soon follow. Amy looks around at the table and slowly stands up and walks outside.

*

Outside the restaurant are several police cars and officers including Detective Baker who glances at Tom several times.

Debbie marches over to Lars and Gibbons and says, "You motherfuckers don't have anything else better to do with your time? He's a good cop. He does a good job!!" She runs over to Russell, holds his face and says, "Don't worry sweetheart. You'll be fine. Everything will be fine." Russell is placed in a squad car. He sits there with his head down.

Baker goes over to Tom. "You should really be careful who you associate with." Baker says.

Tom says, "It….It's not like that. His wife has been calling my wife to get together for lunch for weeks so we just—"

"We never did find him, you know. Smiley I mean." Baker says cutting Tom off. "Wow. He must have slipped through the net." Tom says back.

Baker moves closer to Tom and says, "I doubt it since we did a door to door search, had dogs, helicopters and closed off the streets for a twenty-block radius. No cars in or out. In fact, the only car we let through was yours. And you said you never saw him, right?"

"Yeah." Tom says. "I'm not sure how he got out."

Baker looks at Russell in the squad car with his head down. He then turns back to Tom and says, "It really is a shame when you have to arrest one of your own. Catch you later Tom." Baker slowly walks away, and the police cars drive away. Amy walks over to Tom. They both look at Debbie who now looks more worried then she has in her life.

Amy turns to Tom and says, "He's done, right?" Toms turns back to Amy and says, "Yeah. It's over. The house, cars, fancy restaurants, and clothes. She might be in denial right now though." "You just be careful." Amy says.

Tom steps closer to her and says, "Just be careful?? Did you fucking hear what Baker said? This is what happens when you break the law. You go to fucking jail! Look at Deb's face. That is the reality."

"Well, the main problem with them is they were always flashy. They always liked to be seen. They liked the perception of being more than what they were." Amy says.

Tom says to her, "Oh, you mean like the house we just saw or the clothes you're wearing now? Didn't you say earlier how you like to look the part?" Amy moves a little closer to him and says, "I know you've been stressed out and I know I haven't been very attentive to you. What do you say we go home so I can take care of you? You've had a very rough day."

"Take care of me?" Tom says confused. Amy moves close to him, grabs his hand, and says, "It's hasn't been that long, has it?" She smiles out of the side of her mouth and winks.

Tom snatches his hand away from hers, take a step back and says, "We've been to marriage counseling. I've given you flowers, candy, and spa treatments. I've even surprised you with romantic weekend getaways to Cancun and Jamaica. I have exercised every viable opportunity to save our marriage. Every time I came forward with a way to save it, you took two steps away from me. Out of an act of sheer desperation, I deal under the table for the first time ever and NOW you're feeling amorous? Since that day, I've been looking over my shoulder. I haven't slept well. I can't enjoy my food because of all the shit that's been going on." Amy stands there saying nothing.

Tom just walks away as Amy watches Debbie stand there with her body shaking.

*

Boozer is walking around the reservoir near Lehman College. After a while stops and leans on a car to catch his breath. "Fuck!" he says in between gasps. A BMW slowly drives past him. The car stops and backs up to Boozer. The passenger window lowers, and a young black man named Menace sticks his head out of the window. He has a crucifix around his neck. He says, "Boozer, is that you? Yo man, you're a fucking legend! I used to idolize you and Smiley, Ridley and Big Ben. You were the kings of the area. Look at you now." He says while laughing. "What the fuck happened to you man?"

"Why don't you get the fuck away from me? I'm not in the mood right now!" Boozer snaps and continues to walk down the street. The car jumps the curb right in front of him preventing Boozer from walking. The doors open and four young black men get out. Boozer looks around and sees no one is going to help him.

"I don't want any trouble," Boozer says in a softer tone.

Menace takes out a gun and says, "Too late for that shit motherfucker!" He cracks Boozer in the face with his gun. Boozer falls to the ground and starts breathing very heavily. The four men kick stomp and punch Boozer all over his face and body. "Ahhh! Stop man! Please!!" Boozer begs. Menace holds one hand up, and they all stop beating on Boozer. Menace looks down at him and says, "All I wanted was to pay my respects to someone who paved the way for me and my crew. We came up in these streets harder than you did before us. Not sure if you know bout me but we got some new shit going on and wanted to team up with the old guard before we took over." Boozer looks up slowly at Menace and says, "You can't take over these streets." Menace clenches both fists and asks, "Why the fuck not?" Boozer slowly stands up and wipes the blood off his face. The rest of the men look at each other with wide eyes. Boozer gets close to Menace and says, "You don't have the heart, and you don't have the stomach for it." Menace takes a few steps back with his eyes wide. He looks at his men who look just as confused as he does. After a few moments, Menace narrows his eyes and snarls, "If you ain't gonna show me any respect then fuck all y'all! I'm Menace, and I'm the new king on the throne. You need to fucking retire!"

Boozer looks at him and says, "You don't retire from these streets. The only real way out is if you…" Boozer stops and looks away for a minute.

"Well, you need to do something, 'cause these streets are mine now and don't you fucking forget it!" Menace growls. They all get back in their car. "I better not see you around here again." He says before the car screeches away. Boozer touches his lip and checks for blood. He sits on his car and looks around for a minute then takes out his phone and dials a number,

Smiley's voice – "Yeah. What's up?" There is a pause on the other line. "Hey. Are you there?" He continues.

Boozer takes a deep breath and asks, "We've been in this game for a long time, right? You and me."

"Yes, we have." Smiley asks. There is a pause on the phone then Boozer says, "I know we've had issues over the years, and we've exchanged some words in the past. A few of those

words haven't been friendly. But you always kept my secret."
Boozer says.

"Well, you kept mine, so it was only fair." Smiley responds.

"Even when you had a chance to fuck me over, you never did."
Boozer says.

There is a pause on the other line, and Smiley finally says,
"That wouldn't have benefited either one of us."

"I—I really appreciate that, man." Boozer says faintly. "Where
is all this coming from? What are you saying?" Smiley asks.

"I'm saying thank you." Boozer says as a single tear falls from
his eye. "Life is hard. This game is even harder. We pay so
much attention to all the big bullshit, we really don't appreciate
the little things in life."

"Like what?" Smiley asks. "Doing what we do, you ain't got
the luxury of meeting people you can trust or people you can
call a friend. I guess after all these years; you are the one
person I can call a true friend." Boozer continues.

"Talk to me Booze. What happened?" Smiley asks.

"I found a way out. Of this business. Once and for all." Boozer
says.

There is a pause on the phone, then Smiley asks, "Are your
bags packed?"

"I don't need bags where I'm going. I'm too old for this shit.
We all are." Boozer says. "Speak for yourself. I won't give up.

I can't. I have my photography. That's how I cope." Smiley responds with a slight laugh.

"I've always been jealous of you because you were always braver than me. Much more courageous than I ever was. I could never cope. That's why I started drinking so young. I.....I can't cope anymore." Boozer says.

There is a long pause on the line, and finally Smiley says, "You're sure about this?"

"Yeah. I'm done. You still have those keys I gave you in case of an emergency?" Boozer asks.

"I do." Smiley says. "Where's your wall"?

"You'll find it. Just get there before they do. Peace." Boozer says and hangs up.

Boozer turns his phone off and grabs a rock and destroys it. He then takes out his pills, wallet, keys and his phone and throws it all down the sewer. Boozer then takes a deep breath and then starts walking. He walks faster and faster until he starts running. He runs as fast as he possibly can until he clutches his chest and grabs his arm. He falls to the ground dead.

*

Smiley, wearing a blue suit, is sitting there at a table in a restaurant with Woody with the phone still in his hand. Woody asks, "Who was that?"

Smiley gets up and says, "I have to go." He takes money out of his pocket and throws it on the table and leaves.

Chapter Five

Percival is sleeping in his bed. On the wall next to his bed are huge posters of various Marvel comic book characters. The leg that was shot is elevated on a pillow. His alarm goes off, but he doesn't move.

"Percy! It's time to get up! Come on sweetheart!" His mother yells from downstairs. He slowly opens his eyes and turns off the alarm. He lays there for a minute or two. Taking a deep breath, he slowly and carefully gets out of bed. Once out of bed, he reaches for a cane and walks out of his room toward the bathroom.

*

Percival slowly moves toward the kitchen and sees his mother, Gladys and his father, Philip. Gladys is in her late fifties with a head full of black and white hair. Philip is in his mid-sixties with a bald head and a beer belly. She is drinking a cup of coffee and he is looking at the newspaper. As soon as Gladys sees her son, she puts the coffee cup down goes over to him and wipes some soap off his cheek.

"You missed a spot." Gladys says. "Really, mom?" Percival asks his mother. "Can I make something for you? Eggs? Toast? Anything?" Gladys says to him with a broad smile.

"I'm cool, mom. I'll grab something on the way to school." Percival replies back.

Philip puts down the paper, looks at his wife and says, "I think I left my phone in the bedroom. Can you get it for me, honey? "Absolutely." She walks to the back of the apartment. As soon as she is gone, Philip moves closer to Percival and asks, "You going to school today?"

"I am. It's been a while." Percival responds. Philip has a very disgusted look on his face. Gladys is on her way back to the kitchen and catches Philip pushing Percival up against the wall, grabs his shirt and says, "I don't need you wasting your time." Gladys goes in the kitchen and says, "I think he learned his lesson." She looks at her watch, looks at Philip and says, "You need to go soon. You don't want to be late for work."

Percival looks his father in the eye and says, "Yeah dad. You wouldn't want to be late for work." He lets go of Percival's shirt and goes back to looking at his paper.

*

At school, all of the students are sitting as the teacher, Mr. Beecher hands out the results of their most recent test. He is a black man in his late fifties. Beecher says, "I have to say I am very disappointed with the overall results from the class. There are people here I expected more from. However, the highest grade in the class comes from an unlikely source." He places Percival's test in front of him. His eyes get very wide as he looks at it.

"Percival Tomlinson scored the highest mark in the class." Beecher says. There are moans and groans heard throughout the room.

"How the fuck did he do that?" one student asks.

"He cheated. That's how." Another student responds.

Beecher walks to the front of the class and says, "First of all, language. Second, there is no way anyone could have cheated in this class. To those who didn't do as well as they wanted, there will be a makeup exam given, but Percival will is excused from taking it."

There are more moans and groans, and a student from the back of the class yells, "This sucks!!" The whole class yells and Beecher says, "Knock it off." The bell rings, and the whole class gets up and starts to head out.

"Umm Percival, can you stay for a minute?" Beecher asks. He makes his way to the front of the class, and he and his teacher watch as all of the students leave the class. As soon as the class is empty, he looks at Percival and says, "I don't get it. I don't see you for weeks on end. You don't attend any classes, so I assume you don't know the work. When you do show up without notice to take a test, you score better than anybody else. The work here is obviously too easy. I think you're somehow playing the role of the slow student, but I'm not sure why."

The classroom door is open, and Murdock starts to walk in. He is a ridiculously handsome young man of eighteen years old. "Murdock, can you give us a minute, please?" Beecher says. Murdock stops in his tracks and says, "I'm sorry. I was actually looking for Percy. I'll wait outside." Murdock turns around and leaves the room. Beecher then turns to Percival and says, "I got another call from that specialized school about you. They want to know when they can meet you. They were very impressed with your test results. You were so excited about it a few months ago. What happened?"

"Nothing. Things have changed since then. That's all." Percival says rather blankly. "Like what?" Beecher presses. Percival says nothing and stares blankly into space. Beecher stands up and walks around to him and says, "Please talk to me. You mentioned your father lost his job a while ago. That's when your attitude changed. That's when everything changed."

"Anything else? I have to go." Percival says and starts to walk out. "I know what really happened to your leg." Beecher says very sternly. Percival stops walking and slowly turns around. "I sincerely hope that bullet wound wised you up. These streets are unforgiving. I would hate to be part of a crowd of people in front of the school releasing balloons in your memory. I've done that before for other students. I would hate to do it for you. I don't want you to be a statistic." Beecher continues. Percival looks at him then looks off in the distance. He finally says, "I appreciate your concern. I really do. But I—" Percival stops speaking, and his eyes are getting watery. He sniffs twice, turns and leaves. Beecher reaches for his arm, but Percival pulls away.

He leaves the classroom and Murdock looks at him and smiles, but Percival walks right by him without looking at him. Murdock stands there as Percival goes to his locker. He opens it up and puts some books inside. A classmate, Melanie walks over to him. She is a very voluptuous young woman with long fingernails and red lipstick. An entourage of other young girls follows her. They, in turn, are accompanied by a few boys. One of the boys go over to Melanie and says, "Hey Melanie. You looking real good today girl. Can I take you out?"

Melanie looks at Percival's face and says, "Hey Percy. I heard you got the highest score in the class on that test."

"Where'd you hear that?" Percival responds. Melanie moves closer to him and wipes his eyes. "Allergies are bothering you again?" she asks.

"Umm yeah. I guess so." He says again. She moves closer to him and says, "Listen, since I have to study for the makeup exam, will you help me? You can call it a late birthday present."

"When was your birthday?" He asks. "Two weeks ago." She says and moves very close to him. "You know Melanie; I didn't get you anything."

"I tell you what." She says. "Give me a kiss, and we'll call it even."

"Give you…" Percival says. Melanie puts her arms around his waist and brings her face very close to his. Out of the corner of his eye, he sees Murdock still looking at them from across the hall. Melanie grabs him by the head and pushes his lips into hers. She closes her eyes as their lips touch. He spins her around and kisses her back. He looks over at Murdock and sees him walk away. As soon as he does, Percival lets go of Melanie. She opens her eyes and says, "Wow. We have to go out sometime. When are you going to take me out?"

As he is about to respond, there is some commotion in the hallway. Mr. Kaminsky, a short Jewish man wearing a Kippah walks very briskly over to Mr. Stevenson, a very tall and imposing looking black man. Kaminsky throws a 'Make American Great Again' baseball cap on the floor in front of Stevenson's feet and says, "I believe this belongs to you!" A crowd starts to gather around them, and some of the students have their phones out to record what's happening. Stevenson looks around at the people and then at Kaminsky and yells, "That shit isn't mine!"

"I know it's yours. Just like I know you drew that swastika in the fucking teacher's lounge." Kaminsky yells.

"That's why my president will ship you people back to where you came from. Get the fuck out of my face." Stevenson says. The crowd reacts to that. He pushes Kaminsky who pushes Stevenson back and says, "Don't put your hands on me!"

"Fuck you Jew!" Stevenson yells. They now trade blows and the crowd cheers and records the incident on their phones. The students now surround both teachers as they are fighting and yelling, "Fight! Fight!" Other teachers and security guards are fighting the crowd to move closer to the fighting teachers. Kaminsky gets the upper hand and knocks Stevenson out with a right cross. As Stevenson lies on the ground motionless, the crowd roars in approval. One student yells, "Yo! Mr. K knocked him the fuck out!"

"Now we know what the 'K' stands for." Another student yells out.

Security has reached the teachers in question, and Mr. Kaminsky steps away from an unconscious Stevenson.

Melanie looks around for Percival, but he has blended in the crowd.

*

Later in the day, some students are in the gym locker room. Many are still talking about the fight from earlier and how Mr. K landed the punch that knocked Mr. Stevenson out. Percival comes in the locker room. One kid, Tommy, goes to Percival and says, "Man, you're so fucking lucky you don't have to take gym." Another kid, Rob gets very close to Percival and says in a low faint voice, "I know what you've been doing, man. I need to do something like that. I need to make some real money.

This shit I make as a stock boy at the supermarket is nothing. Hook me up with a contact so I can get in."

Percival looks at Rob and says, "I don't really make that much money. My situation is a little different." Murdock walks in the locker room and looks at Percival but says nothing. He brushes past Percival, but as he does, he sticks a note in the back pocket of his jeans. "So, you'll hook me up? Please?" Rob asks Percival who touches the back pocket where the note is and replies, "I'll see what I can do." Percival bends over slightly and slowly walks out of the locker room. As soon as he leaves the area, he digs in his back pocket for the note Murdock left. He smiles slightly and leaves.

*

After school, Percival is walking through a nearby park. He sees Murdock sitting at a picnic table under a tree. Murdock sees his angry face.

"What's the matter?" Murdock asks.
Percival struggles to sit down at the table. "You can't do shit like that?" He yells at Murdock.

Murdock helps Percival put his legs under the table more comfortably. He looks at Percival with slight annoyance and a smile and says, "Like what? What did I do?" Percival looks at Murdock, and his body starts to shake a little. He opens his mouth, but no words come out. Finally, he says, "I…you….we…"

"And how was that kiss with Melanie?" Murdock asks with a smile on one side of his face. Percival starts to cry slightly and says, "I don't understand. Melanie is the finest girl in school. I mean she's fucking drop dead gorgeous. Every dude in school wants her. Every girl in school wants to be her. I even see some teachers checking her out. I'm the only one she seems to be interested in. She is always flirting with me and putting her hands on me, but when she kissed me today, I honestly felt nothing. I really did. How can I feel nothing for her but a boy puts a note in my back pocket and I have to run out of the locker room stooped over to hide my erection? How?

"That's because you're gay, sweetheart." Murdock says tenderly wiping Percival's tears. "Just admit it. You'll feel better." He continues.

"But I can't be gay!" Percival continues. Murdock moves closer to Percival which makes him look around to see if anyone sees them. "If I kissed you right now, what would you do? Push me away? Punch me?" Murdock asks.

Percival slides away from Murdock a little and says, "Are you crazy? You kissing me with all the shit going on in the country right now? Gays, Sikhs, Jews, and Blacks are being attacked randomly nationwide. That's not a good idea. Did you hear someone drew a swastika in the teachers' bathroom?"

"The teachers' bathroom??" Murdock asks.

"Yup. And those bathrooms don't have keys. They need key codes. Which means only a teacher can get in." Percival continues. "I guess that's why Kaminsky and Stevenson were fighting."

"I heard it wasn't much of a fight. Stevenson just stood there, and Mr. K laid his dumb ass out." Murdock says with a laugh.

"Well, he's always been a low-key supporter of those initiatives. Besides, he hates Jews and has made no attempt to hide that. I can't believe how stupid he is. And he's a fucking teacher." Percival says.

"He's gay too." Murdock says. Percival turns to him with his eyes very wide and exclaims, "He's—really? He's black and gay? That doesn't even make sense."

"I mean they pay him to shape young minds." Murdock exclaims.

Percival turns to Murdock and says, "Did you hear someone ripped off Safa's hijab last week and says she's going to get shipped back to Morocco? These are scary times."

"So, you'd rather run and hide back in the closet than accept who you are?" Murdock asks.

Percival looks at Murdock then looks away and says, "Am I really?? I—I…" He starts crying again and says, "You must think I'm a real pussy for crying like this."

Murdock puts his hand on Percival and says, "Saying you're a pussy puts a very negative female connotation on that word. Besides, this isn't the real you. That tough act is just an act. I saw through that when we were in elementary school. But you're filled with self-hate. You see other gay couples, and it makes you angry because you think that's how other people see you. You lash out violently, and you have to stop that. You really do." Murdock wipes more of Percival's tears and asks, "Now tell me what's going on with you and what kind of trouble you're in."

Percival glances over and him and turns away saying, "I really can't. It's complicated." Percival puts his head in his hands. Murdock moves closer to him and says, "If you keep that sad look on your face, you'll force me to do something to cheer you up."

"Like what?" Percival sneers. Murdock then lifts up Percival's shirt and starts to tickle his stomach. Percival turns to him and says, "No. Stop. I'm not in the mood." Murdock continues to tickle him, and Percival then turns away from him and laugh loudly. "Seriously, stop. You're going to give me another erection." He says through his laughter.

Murdock looks down at his crotch and says, "Looks like you already have one." They look at each other and then they kiss. "You know how long I've wanted to do that?" Percival asks.

"Let's go. It's getting late." Murdock says. "I can't walk back to my house stooped over. I have to wait until my erection calms down." Percival says very embarrassedly.

Murdock smiles slightly at him and starts to unbuckle his pants. Percival jumps a little and looks around to see if anyone is watching. He looks at Murdock and says, "I'm a virgin."

"Me too." Murdock replies.

"What do you mean? You told me last summer about all the ass you got." Percival states. Murdock thinks for a minute, starts laughing and says, "Oh! For some reason, my uncle decided to move to Scotland. We went to visit him last summer. He runs a donkey farm." Percival starts to laugh, and Murdock continues to unzip his pants.

"It was you, you know." Percival says. Murdock just looks at him. "I didn't want to transfer to that special school because I knew if I did, I wouldn't get to see you every day. I don't know what I would do if I couldn't see you every day."

Murdock touches his face and kisses him again. "We are about to commit a sex act in a public place. That's against the law. You can't make any noise. OK?" He says. Percival nods obediently. Murdock gives Percival a hand job under the table. Percival moans lightly and ejaculates quickly.

"I'm so sorry." Percival says meekly. "It's OK. That means you enjoyed it." Murdock says. He kisses Percival again. He looks at Murdock and says, "That means I'm definitely gay." As they both get up to leave the park, Murdock takes out baby wipes from his bag and wipes his hands, and Percival fixes his pants. Percival looks at him and asks, "You carry baby wipes with you?" Murdock slightly smiles and replies, "I like to be prepared."

*

They are walking down the street. "The fuck am I going to do now?" Percival wonders. "I think you should transfer to that special school, so you challenge yourself. We can figure the rest out later. It's not the end of the world if we don't see each other every day." Murdock says.

"It's not that simple." Percival says as he rolls his eyes and shakes his head. He turns to Percival and says, "But you need to stop running with that gang. You already got shot once. These streets will kill you. Assholes like Ridley and Boozer don't give a fuck if you live or die. But I do and so does your mother."

Percival looks straight ahead and sees his mother Gladys walking very quickly towards them. She looks distraught. "Shit." Percival says. Murdock looks down the street and Gladys. "I didn't know it was that late." Murdock says.

Gladys reaches them, and Percival can see that she has been crying and she has bruises on her face. Percival lightly touches her face and says, "What happened? Did he hit you again? I'll kill that motherfucker!" Gladys holds his hand, squeezes it and says, "No. It's not that. It's worse. Much worse." Percival looks in his mother's eyes and says, "Shit."

"You need to come home with me right now." Gladys says urgently.

Murdock steps closer to them and says, "You need backup?" "No. If I need you, I will call you." Percival says. They touch hands, and Murdock watches as Percival and Gladys walk down the street.

"So, was that your boyfriend?" Gladys says without looking at Percival. Percival stops his mother from walking and says, "How did you know? I never let on that I was…"

Gladys touches her son's face and says, "I'm your mother, and a mother always knows. In life, we all have our parts to play. And right now, I need you to play the tough defender. Please." Tears start to form from her eyes. "I'll do whatever I have to do." Percival says. They continue walking.

*

They get to their apartment and find the door unlocked and slightly ajar. They walk in, and Percival finds furniture knocked over, broken dishes on the floor and in the living room, Philip is on his knees buck naked. Standing around him are Big Ben, Ridley, Woody, and Lando. Big Ben and Ridley are holding guns to Philip's head. Lando comes around and holds a gun to Glady's head. Percival gets right in Lando's face and says, "Take that fucking gun off my mother!"

"Where the fuck you been?" Ridley asks. "I was at school. What fucking difference does it makes now. What the fuck is going on here? Why you all here?" Percival yells.

"Boozer's dead." Ridley says.

"What??" Percival says shocked. "How? How did he die?"

"Do I look like a fucking medical examiner? He's dead, and I need to find out if he had any shit in his place. I think he might have been holding out." Ridley says.

"Holding out what?" Percival asks.

"That's what I need you to find out for me." Ridley says.

"How long have you been working for him?" Gladys asks. Percival looks at Philip and says, "Oh you didn't tell her?"

"Tell me what?" Gladys asks. Philip doesn't say anything. She gets right in his face and yells, "Tell me what??"

Percival looks at his father who now has a look of embarrassment and shame. He then looks at his mother and says, "He lost his job three months ago. We were behind on our bills. He went to Ridley and offered him my services in exchange for money to pay rent and food."

Gladys looks confused and says, "Wait. What?"

Ridley looks at Gladys and says, "I own your son now. Your husband sold him to me."

Gladys marches over to Philip and kicks him repeatedly in the head, and Big Ben has to restrain her.

"How can you do that? How can you do that to your own son?" Gladys yells.

"I figured the boy needed to toughen up. Considering his nature and all." Philip says. Percival looks around slightly embarrassed, but no one says anything. Gladys takes a step toward him and says, "What does his nature have anything to do with you being his father? So where have you been going for the last three months?"

"He plays his numbers, he shoots dice, and he goes to the casino." Percival says.

Gladys gets Big Ben to let go him her, and she walks over to Ridley and says, "I had no idea this was going on."

"I know you didn't." Ridley says.

Gladys gets down on her knees and says, "I am begging for my son's life. Please let him stay with me. What will it take?"

"About fifteen thousand dollars. We gave your husband ten and then there was interest." Ridley says.

"I don't have that kind of money." Gladys says. "Is there anything here of value you can take?" She pleads.

"Nah. We already checked. Look, this is business." Gladys looks at Ridley with tears in her eyes and says, "Is there any other way?" Ridley and the rest of his crew take out their guns. Ridley helps his mother up from being on her knees and says with a stern voice, "We can't let him go. We told him everything. He knows all our secrets. Now, the only way we can let him go is if we kill all of you right now and put it down as a loss in the books. But I don't wanna do that. He shouldn't be out here. These streets ain't no fucking joke. But your husband came to us with an offer, and I took it. Take it up with him." Ridley says. He checks the time on his phone and says, "We have to go. Let's hit it Percy."

Percival goes to his mother and says, "I'll do whatever I need to do. I'll see you later." He gives Gladys a kiss, and they all leave the apartment. Philip who is still lying on the floor from the kicks Gladys gave him slowly stands up. He looks at Gladys not sure of what do say. He watches as she walks into the bedroom. He hears rustling and clothes being handled and clicking noises. She comes out of the bedroom with a suitcase full of her clothes. Some of which are sticking out of the suitcase as she passes him in the living room and heads towards the front door. She takes out her house keys and throws them on the floor. She opens the apartment door and walks out without closing it.

Chapter Six

Ridley and Big Ben are sitting in the front seat of a large SUV. Percival and Woody are in the back seat. They are parked outside Boozer's apartment. Everyone in the vehicle takes out their guns. Ridley turns around to everyone and says, "Everyone ready? I don't want any noise, but I don't want to take any chances either. If you see him, put two in his head. You got it?" They all nod. "Let's do this." Ridley says as they all put their guns away and get out of the car. They take a look around the area and walk into the building. Ridley presses the elevator, and the door opens. "Big Ben and I will take the elevator. You two take the stairs." He continues. Ridley and Big Ben enter the elevator, and the door closes. Woody and Ridley look at each other then walk up the stairs.

They all meet outside of Boozer's apartment and see the door is already ajar. "Shit!" Big Ben says and looks at Ridley who has a scowl on his face. They all enter with their guns out and see the place has been completely ransacked. Cushions from the couch and chairs have been sliced open.

"Spread out. See if he missed anything." Ridley says. Ridley goes in the bedroom and sees the mattress cut open, clothes from the closets and dresser draws are thrown all over the floor. There are large holes in the walls. "Fuck you, Smiley." He mumbles.

"Yo Ridley." Big Ben bellows from another room.

Ridley walks to the kitchen and sees the cabinets are all open with lots of dishes carefully placed on the counter. "Smiley wrecked this place. Is there anything here?" Ridley asks. They all look away and a little embarrassed. "What?" Ridley asks. He looks at Big Ben who looks away. "What!?! Did Smiley leave anything for us?? Ridley yells at everyone. "He did leave something." Big Ben says. Ridley moves closer to him. "What? What did he leave?" Ridley demands. Big Ben slowly open the fridge to show Ridley a huge turd on a plate with a note on it that reads, 'Ridley, eat this.' Ridley slams the fridge door hard and says, "Fuck you, Smiley!! Why the fuck does that smell so bad?" He says. Woody looks behind the fridge and says, "Looks like he unplugged it." Ridley and Big Ben look at each other and pulls the fridge out and sees a huge piece of cardboard cut to fit the back of the fridge and painted the same color. Ridley looks at Percival and motions him to the fridge. Percival jumps behind the fridge and sees the cardboard is loose. He pulls it completely off and sees indentations of money that covers the entire length of the fridge. Percival looks at Ridley and says, "Looks like he took it all." Ridley sucks his teeth and turns away. Percival looks down and sees a hundred-dollar bill ripped in half. He hands it to Ridley who looks at it and crumbles it to the floor. Big Ben looks at Percival and asks, "Anything else in there?" Percival looks around and sees an old laundromat ticket in the corner. He hands it to Ridley. Big Ben goes around to Ridley and looks at the ticket. "Isn't this the place where his bitch works?" Ridley asks. Big Ben snaps his fingers and says, "That Chink was Boozer's side piece. He's been fucking her for years." Ridley looks at Big Ben and widens his eyes. Big Ben smileys slightly and nods slowly. "Shit. Well, we need to check her out." Ridley says then turns to Percival. "Percy!" He yells. Percival jumps out from behind the fridge and stands in front of Ridley almost at attention and says, "Yes. Ridley!"

"Calm the fuck down kid. This ain't the fucking military." Ridley says. "Ben, Woody and I will go to the laundromat to talk to this bitch. I'm sending you and two other guys to Smileys place. You kill him and bring back all of the shit he took. You do that; you're free to go." Percival smiles a little and asks, "Are you serious?"

"You get to go home." Ridley says. Percival smiles to himself. Big Ben pushes him up against the wall and barks, "The fuck are you smiling about? Smiley ain't no fucking joke. He got skills." Percival pushes him off and says, "So do I." He starts to leave when Ridley grabs him by the arm and says, "Don't fuck this up. This is your chance to wipe the fucking slate clean. OK?" Percival nods enthusiastically then leaves. Ridley looks around and says, "Let's get the fuck outta here." They all leave.

Ridley, Big Ben, and Woody walk into the laundromat and find out the place is pretty much empty. They see Joanna sitting at her desk in the back reading a newspaper about Boozer's death. They all walk over to her and Ridley asks, "Hey. You speak English?" She just smiles and nods. Big Ben looks at the page of the newspaper Joanna is looking at and sees Boozer's picture. "He's dead. You know that, right? Joanna looks at Big Ben and says, "Boozer dead. He no more. Sad." Ridley looks at Joanna and says, "You were fucking him, right?" Joanna looks at Ridley and smiles wide and says, "Fuck. Yes! Boozer have big black cock. Good fuck."

Big Ben says, "Let's go. She don't know shit." Ridley looks at her and says, "She knows exactly what the fuck I'm saying." Joanna starts yelling something in Chinese and banging in the newspaper. Ridley puts up both hands and says, "OK. OK. We're leaving. Let's go." They all leave. As soon as they do, Joanna slowly gets up and goes to the door to make sure they are gone. Once they are, she goes back to the newspaper with Boozer's picture. She tenderly touches the picture and says, "Fuck."

Smiley is in the bedroom of his apartment counting the money he got from Boozer's place.

In the kitchen, a window slowly opens, and a man climbs inside. In the bedroom, Smiley looks at his mobile device and sees the silent alarm has been activated. He smiles at this and a pair of gloves with short knives in the back of it. He also takes a remote control for the sound system.

Percival is in the kitchen with the other two thugs. Both men are huge and formidable. "Split up. Find him and kill him." Percival whispers. All three of them go in different parts of the apartment.

One of the men walks down a long hallway with a closet door on the side of it. As soon as he passes in front of the door, loud booming and thunderous music plays over the sound system. The thug jumps with fright from the noise. "AHHH!" he yells. As soon as he yells, a closet door opens wide enough for Smiley to stick his arm out with a gun and shoot the thug at point blank range. Smiley grabs the thug by the collar before he falls to the ground and gently places him on the floor. Smiley then turns the music off. He goes back into his bedroom when the other thug comes from behind him and knocks the gun from Smiley's hand. He throws a punch to which Smiley evades easily and punches him square in the testicles. The thug screams in pain and yells, "Motherfucker!!" He throws Smiley up against the wall. Smiley extends the small knives on the back knuckles of the gloves he is wearing and punches the thug in the chest. He touches his chest and sees blood; he is enraged and rushes Smiley and pins him against the wall. Smiley punches him repeatedly in his sides until the thug lets go. Once he does, Smiley punches him in the face and slashes him across his cheek. Lots of blood start pouring out of his face. The thug holds his cheek in place because the cut Smiley gave him is so deep, his cheek is almost hanging off of his face. He throws a punch, but Smiley evades it easily and punches him in the ribcage on both sides of his body. The thug screams in pain. "Yo Percival!!" the thug pleads. Percival gets there in time to see Smiley throw the thug to the ground and starts punching him and creating small cuts all over his face and body. "Fucking help me Percy!!" the thug yells. Percival starts to come forward, but Smiley grabs his gun and shoots at Percival barely missing his head. Percival falls to the floor ducking the shot. "That was a warning shot. Don't you fucking move, Percival!!" Smiley yells. He sits there and watches as Smiley continues to beat the other thug. Smiley grabs the thug by the throat and asks, "Who sent you?" The thug says nothing. "Really??" Smiley says to him.

"Fuck you." The thug finally says to which Smiley stabs him in the throat. The thug goes limp, and Smiley slowly stands up and looks at Percival who now has urinated on himself. His whole body is shaking as Smiley gets closer. He points his gun at Percival's head and asks, "Hey Percival! How the leg?" Smiley grabs Percival and slams him up against the wall. "Don't move." Smiley says. He walks back in the bedroom and returns with the same camera Percival held earlier. "Remember this one? This is the one you slammed on the table when you were going through my bag." Smiley says.

"Please don't kill me!!" Percival pleads.

Smiley smiles at him and says, "I'm going to ask you a few questions. How you answer those questions will determine if I shoot you with this." Smiley moves the advance lever on the camera to advance the film inside. "Or with this." Smiley cocks the gun.

"Are you ready?" Smiley asks. Percival has a look of horror and fright on his face. Smiley smiles at him.

*

Tom is outside Jason's apartment, he knocks on the door, and a huge and muscular man named Rich opens the door. Rich looks at Tom up and down and says, "He's been expecting you." He leads Tom into the living room where he finally sees Jason. He's a white man in his late sixties in a wheelchair with an oxygen tank on the side and breathing tubes in his nose. Jason's breathing is very labored, and he's very gaunt. Jason is holding a newspaper article. He reads, "Tom Simms has built a long and illustrious career in law enforcement amassing a multitude of accolades, awards, commendations, and citations. Seen here with the Mayor, Police Commissioner, and PBA President, as he receives yet another award. Set to retire soon, he was asked how does it feel to be one of the most celebrated and respected police officers in the history of the NYPD. Tom said and I quote, 'I have always been humbled by my law enforcement career and just do what I feel I was born to do.' End quote." Jason lowers the paper and looks Tom square in the eye and says, "Do you know why I became a cop?"

"Jason, I have no idea." Tom replies. "Sit down." Jason says. Tom sits on a nearby chair.

Jason moves his wheelchair closer to Tom and says, "I never knew my father. He fucked my mother, left and she never saw him again. I don't even have a picture of him. I could have walked by him in the street or arrested him in my career and never would have known. My mother worked two jobs waiting tables at two diners in the Bronx. What I'm saying is, we were poor. I mean really poor. So poor we had to live in the projects on welfare because having two jobs working for tips still wasn't enough. You know what it's like to be a white family in a black neighborhood? We fucking stood out like tits on a bull. I was picked on, bullied and beat up every day. There was this one guy who always took pleasure out of kicking my ass. One day I decided to stick up for myself. I said to him, 'Leave me the fuck alone!' And while he and his crew were punching and stomping all over me, one question kept coming to my mind. You know what that was?" He asks. Tom shuffles in his chair and says, "I can imagine."

"I was wondering what it must feel like to put a nigger's head through a plate glass window." Jason says without hesitation. "I worked hard in school and took the test right after I graduated. My third day on the job, I got my answer. And it felt fucking great. I wound up patrolling the same projects I grew up in. Can you fucking believe it? Those same assholes that bullied me were still there. This time, when they saw me, they walked the other way. I built a name for myself ever since. I was the king on the throne." Tom says, "Yeah, and look at you now." Jason looks at himself and says, "I know. The bullet in my spine is killing me. The doctors say I have a year. Maybe less. But that's not why I called you here. I know you killed a man in cold blood." Tom raises his eyebrows and shifts uncomfortably in his seat.

"How do you know that?" Tom asks.

"I know everything." Jason replies.

"Look. That bastard forced me to shoot that guy. Did you know that?" Tom asks with desperation in his voice.

"Of course, I knew that." Jason says back. "You waited this long in your career to take a bribe? Jason says while he laughs so hard, he starts to cough. Rich starts to come over, but Jason stops him. Tom says very nervously, "Look, t-that was a one-time deal, I was….am having some problems at home and I—" Jason starts laughing and coughing even more.

"Do you realize what an advantage this is for us? No one would ever suspect you. You of all people! You now have a license to steal and kill, but you have to do this right." Jason hands Tom a tiny pistol and says, "Here, take this. Keep it on you at all times. Never let them take it from you. If they try, blast them. Those are hollow point bullets in that gun and will blow their fucking heads off. Never hesitate to take what's yours.   Like this one asshole who's been indirectly working for me for years. I started to notice after each deal; the count was a little short. Not by much but enough for me to notice. Actually, there were two assholes, but one died recently. But I'm taking care of this other asshole tonight. His name is Travis."

"I don't know who that is." Tom says looking very confused as he straps the small pistol to his ankle. Jason leans forward and says, "You probably know him by his street name, Smiley. The one who gave you that money to escape. Remember?"

Tom looks at the clock on the wall. Jason notices this and says, "He's probably dead already." "How much did he take?" Tom asks. "More than enough." Jason responds back. They sit there in silence for a few seconds until Tom says, "You know Russell got arrested earlier today, right?" "I heard. Fucking idiot." Jason responds with a huff and a shake of the head. Tom takes a very long look at Jason and finally asks, "You had something to do with it, didn't you?"

Jason adjusts himself in his chair and says, "He was getting sloppy and making mistakes. And his wife was way too flashy. She was always buying something new. That kind of stuff always attracts attention. Do you want to know why Russell really wanted to get together with you? Tom shakes his head 'no.'

"It wasn't because of your wife. Or his wife. He wanted you to legitimize him." Jason says. "He knew IAD was closing in on him so he figured if he could associate himself with The Tom Simms, they might back off. But now that I have you on my side, it's much better. A veteran who knows the streets extremely well and who has street smarts. We can't be stopped. Tell me, how are those home repairs going?" Jason continues. Tom's mouth slightly opens, and he raises his eyebrows. "How did you know that? Who told you?" Tom asks very nervously. "I told you." Jason responds coolly. "I know everything. Now you need to be careful. Don't be stupid like Russell." "What do you mean?" Tom asks. Jason leans forward a little in Tom's direction and says, "Paying for a job that big in cash is not a good idea. It draws attention. The wrong kind of attention which is the kind of attention we don't need. Don't fucking do it again."

Tom adjusts himself and says, "Who do you think you are? Don't talk to me like that." Jason sits back in his chair. He smiles at Rich who smiles back. Jason glares at Tom and says, "Don't start talking tough. It's not you at all." Tom looks very nervously at Jason and says, "Look, that was a one-time deal. I'm not cut out for this kind of thing." Jason laughs slightly and says, "You mean cut out for taking money under the table but not for the consequences afterwards. It's way too late for that. And you don't really have a choice." They stare at each other.

His house phone rings. Rich looks at Jason who motions his head towards the phone. Rich walks over and answers it. "Hello?" Rich says. "Who are you again? Yeah, hang on a second." Rich hands the phone to Jason. "It's the new guy." Jason grabs the phone and says, "Percy? Where are you?"

"I'm across the street. Look out the window." Percival says. Jason rolls over to the window and sees him standing across the street holding his leg. There's a huge duffle bag on the ground next to him. Jason sees the bag and says, "Is that it? What the fuck are you waiting for? Bring it up." "I can't." Percival says. "He shot me again in the same leg. I have to get to a doctor. I don't want to track blood on your floor. Tell your man to come down and get it." Percival continues.

"Good idea. Don't track that shit in my house. Don't move your ass. Rich will be down in two minutes. I'll stay on the phone with you." Jason says. He turns to Rich and says, "Go down there and get my money." Rich goes to the door, opens it and immediately gets shot twice in the face by a silenced pistol from Smiley. He is wearing a pair of dress pants and a long sleeve dress shirt. Rich falls back in the apartment dead and Tom and Jason both jump back in shock and fear. Smiley quietly enters the apartment and closes the door while pointing the gun at Jason. He glances at Tom who doesn't say anything. Smiley reaches for the phone. "I'll take that." He says to Jason with a smile. Jason slowly hands him the phone. "I'm in." Smiley says on the phone.

"We good?" Percival asks.

"I ever see you again; I'll kill you." Smiley says as he hangs up the phone and drops it on the floor. He smiles at Jason. Jason looks him in the eye and says, "Travis." Smiley looks back and says, "Clayton."

Tom looks at them both as his eyes widen. He walks right in front of Jason and asks, "You're Clayton?" "Why don't you go in the second bedroom right now." Smiley says to Tom while never taking his eyes on Jason.

"Why? What's in there?" Tom asks. "Just do it." Smiley says. Tom looks at Jason then looks back at Smiley who nods to him. Tom starts to walk to the back bedrooms, and Jason says, "Tom if you know what's good for you, don't go back there." Jason tries to move his wheelchair in Tom's direction, and Smiley prevents him from turning. He presses the gun to Jason's head until he stops fidgeting in the chair.

In the bedroom, Tom looks around and sees it appears like a standard bedroom; there are a bed, two-night stands, and two dresser drawers. One is much taller than the other. He yells out, "So? I'm here. I don't see anything so special."

"There are two dressers in the room with you. Open the taller one." Smiley yells back. Tom goes to the taller one and pulls one of the drawers out. The entire front of the dresser opens as a whole door which is actually a refrigerator. There are about four shelves with all have pints and vials of blood. "Hey! Tom yells out. "Who's fucking blood is this?" There is no response. "Did you fucking hear me?!?!" Tom screams louder.

"Now open the small dresser. They keep him in the freezer." Smiley yells from the living room. "They keep who in the freezer?? Who's in there?" Tom says very nervously.

Tom walks slowly to the other dresser. He puts his hand on it then takes it off. He puts his hand on it and opens the freezer door. A lot of the frosty mist comes out first making it hard to him to see anything. He waves the mist away until it thins out. When it does, Tom sees a severed head and two severed hands in their own zip lock bag. "The fuck?" Tom says. He slams the door closed and marches back in the living room where Smiley is still holding the gun on Jason. "Who is that?" Tom demands. Jason doesn't say anything. Tom looks at Smiley and says, "You know who that is?" Smiley looks at Tom and says, "That's Clayton." Tom just looks at Smiley. "What-what do you mean that's Clayton?"

Smiley looks at Jason and says, "Clayton was his chief tormentor when he was growing up. He was trying to make a name for himself and rising up in the ranks fairly quickly. He did a long stretch inside, and by the time Clayton got out, Jason was already a cop. Jason always had Clayton on his radar and followed him. One night, he caught Clayton alone and killed him. But he didn't just kill him. He took his clothes, his head, his hands and drained several pints of blood. Whenever he felt the police were closing in on him, he would use a footprint from Clayton's boot or a snippet from his hair or—"

"Or a drop of his blood." Tom continues.

"Exactly. The police were literally chasing a ghost for years." Smiley moves forward to Jason and says, "And this all would have continued if he hadn't gotten caught with his hand in the cookie jar, went to jail and lost his job on the force."

Jason slowly makes a move toward a gun hidden in his wheelchair but Smiley grabs it and shoots him in the shoulder. "Fuck!" Jason screams and holds his shoulder. "What the fuck?!" He yells.

"You tried to kill me." Smiley says. "I knew you were stealing from me for years. You forget I told you I would come after anyone who tried to cross me." Jason says. Smiley looks at Jason and says, "And you forget what I said. I told you if you ever came at me, I would finish what I started. Jason stares at him with his mouth open.

"I never really liked wearing masks, but I thought it was the best way. I wanted to show you how serious I was. That's why I killed your wife first. I never intended to kill you; just slow you down." Smiley says as he points his gun to Jason's head. "Holy shit," Tom says. Jason sinks in his chair a little and says, "You? You did this? You put me in this fucking chair?" He just smiles at Jason and says, "And now I'm going to put you in the fucking ground." Jason starts sweating a lot and is looking at Smiley very nervously. "D-don't kill me. I'll tell you where the money is." Jason pleads.
"It's in the fake wall in the back of the closet in the master bedroom." Smiley says. Jason now smiles and says, "Now I know why they call you Smiley."

"No, you don't." Smiley says back and shoots Jason point blank in his head. Smiley pushes Jason's body on the floor. Tom takes out his gun and points it at Smiley and says, "You're under arrest."

"Hold that thought." Smiley says. He turns and walks to the master bedroom. Tom turns with him still pointing his gun. Tom hears punching and banging. A few minutes later Smiley comes out with two huge duffle bags. Tom is still pointing his gun at Smiley. Smiley puts one of the bags down and says, "This bag is filled with money. Jason is dead, and Clayton is dead twice. People are going to be looking for him and this money, and none of those people are cops. You want to stick around?" Smiley opens the door and leaves. Tom lowers his gun, looks at Jason's body then looks at the duffle bag. He puts his gun away, picks up the bag and follows Smiley out of the apartment.

Chapter Seven

Tom goes to Smiley who is standing in the vestibule of the building staring at the street. Tom looks at him and says, "How the fuck do we get out of here? There are probably cameras everywhere, and it's late at night. This is New York City! Smiley turns to Tom, smiles and says, "This is the Bronx." He takes out his cell phone and goes to a number that says, 'Taxi, Taxi.' He dials it and says, "Taxi, Taxi. I need an out right away. Don't take the main streets. Go parallel. I'm at Jason's." He hangs up.

Tom looks at him. Smiley looks back at Tom and says, "Most of the cameras in New York are in Manhattan. The ones in the Bronx are only at major points. But you can still avoid cameras if you travel on secondary roads that run parallel to the main streets." Tom looks at him and laughs a little. "I never thought of that." Tom says.

A car pulls up, and two Jamaican men are inside. Horace is driving and sitting in the passenger side is a man named Nigel. Smiley and Tom get in the car. Nigel turns around and says, "Who the fuck is this cop?" Tom sits up a little alarmed. "How did you know I was —"

"Don't worry. He's on our side. Use the side streets and take me to the Gardens." Smiley says interrupting Tom and reassuring Nigel and Horace. Tom leans toward Smiley and asks, "You think going to Madison Square Garden is a good idea?"

"I didn't say Madison Square Garden. I said the Gardens. Horace? Let's try really hard not to get stopped, OK?"

Horace starts the car moving. He looks at Smiley in the rear-view mirror and says, "Trust me. Now that people are trying to make America great again, I don't want to run the risk of getting caught and deported."

"Again." Nigel says.

"Yeah, again." Horace repeats. "So, this trip will cost extra. You know how it is." "Yes. And the price of freedom is always high." Smiley says. He looks around the car and asks, "New ride, Horace?" Smiley asks.

"Yup. The seller had two cars from Eagle. The Dude and the Freedom. He wanted me to buy both, but I liked the Freedom better."

"He say why he was selling?" Smiley asks.

"I heard some of those cars are shit." Nigel says. "I was thinking about buying an Eagle." Tom says. They get to a red light, and Horace turns to Tom and says, "Don't. These cars are having serious issues lately." Tom leans forward to Horace and asks, "What kind of issues?" As soon as the light changes green the car starts to move, then it sputters and stalls out. The engine dies. Horace and Nigel both look at Tom. "These kinds of issues." Nigel replies.

Smiley punches the car seat and says, "Are you fucking kidding? This is the last thing we need." Tom looks around and asks, "What do we do now?" Tom asks. Smiley checks his watch and says, "Fuck do we do now? Can't call a tow with this shit on us. We have to call someone we can trust. Horace and Nigel look at each other and then Horace takes out his phone. Smiley looks at him and asks, "You know someone good?" Horace looks back and replies, "I know someone even better."

Benjamin Wilkins and Preeti Hapuarachi are sitting in her apartment having dinner. He is in his late thirties and stands a towering six foot four inches tall and weighs two hundred seventy-eight pounds. She is an Indian woman in her early thirties. She has long thick jet-black hair and a small cut on her face from a knife. She is very tall and curvy.

"So, tell me again how you were able to get the car running again." Preeti asks. Ben looks at her and says, "Because I'm fucking talented." They both laugh. "Actually, I found out something very interesting about the wiring." His phone rings. Ben looks at it and answers, "What's up Horace?"

"Yo, Benji! I'm in a fucking bind, man. I'm in some really deep shit. You told me to call you if I had any issues with cars from Eagle. I got a problem." Horace says. Ben stands up and says, "I'm on my way. Text me exactly where you are. I'll be there as soon as I can." Ben hangs up and starts to grabs his coat, tools, and electrical tape. "Another problem with a car from Eagle?" Preeti asks.

"Seems that way." Benjamin says as he heads to the front door.

"How long will you be?" Preeti asks.

"I have no idea. Hopefully not too long." Ben says.

"I might pop over to Bea's joint and check out her clothes." Preeti says. They kiss, and Ben says, "I'll see you tonight." Ben leaves.

Horace, Nigel, Smiley, and Tom are still sitting in the car. Smiley has his hand on his gun looking around nervously for anything out of the ordinary. A car approaches and stops in front of them. Benjamin gets out and slowly approaches the car. Horace gets out and shakes his hand.

Yo Ben!" Horace says, "You look like you lost some weight." Benjamin stares at the car and says, "I've been fucking stressed over this Eagle car shit. What happened?"

"Not sure. It just fucking died on me." Horace says. Nigel says, "Yo, I heard shit like this has been happening to a lot of people. Some people have even been killed. Like that lady from before?"

"Virginia." Ben says meekly. "Oh shit. You knew her." Nigel says. "In a way. You got a jack? We need to jack this car up." Ben says.

Horace turns to Nigel and says, "Nigel, get your ass out of the car and help Benji."

"In fact, I need everyone out of the car right now." Benjamin says as he takes off his coat. Inside the car, Smiley says, I'm not getting out. He has to do this with me in here." Benjamin walks over and leans over to the back seat where Smiley and Tom are. I need to car empty to make it easier to lift up." Smiley stares at him saying nothing. "The longer you take, the longer it takes for me to finish doing what I have to do." Tom gets out of the car and says, "Good enough for me." Benjamin looks over at Smiley and says, "The car would be lighter if you got out." Smiley glares at him and says, "You can do this with me in here. Get started." "First of all, I don't fucking work for you." Benjamin says. "Second, the car is still to heavy with you in it. It will only take five minutes." Tom pokes his head in the window and says, "People are going to be looking for us and they won't be cops. You said it yourself. Get out of the fucking car so we can get this done." Smiley turns to Benjamin then back to Tom. He slowly opens the door and gets out. He stands behind Tom and takes his gun out. Nigel takes out the jack and lifts the vehicle as Ben takes off his coat. Smiley leans over to Tom and says, "What the fuck is taking so long?" Tom says, "I don't know. But I do know if you want to get out of this, you can't make a scene." He looks down and sees his gun. "Do yourself a favor and put your thing away."

Once the jack has lifted the car high enough, Ben gets on the floor and goes under it. He takes out his mini flashlight and sees the burnt wires in the same place as the other cars. "Son of a bitch." Ben grumbles. He takes out the electrical tape but sees something wedged in near the wires that are shining in the light. Ben moves the light closer to the object. He tries to reach in there, but his hand is too large. From his pocket, he pulls out a wrench and knocks the object out of the car and onto the street. It makes a clanging sound and bounces a little before settling near Ben's head. "What the—" he says silently. Ben slowly picks up the gold ring and holds it close to the light. He sees it has an inscription on it in a foreign language. Ben's eyes get very wide, and he covers his mouth to keep himself from gasping out loud.

"Everything OK under there, Benji?" Horace asks.

"Uhh yeah. Yeah. I'm fine. Almost done here. Give me a minute." Ben says out loud to Horace but staring intently at the ring. He takes out his electrical tape and secures the wires. "Try it now." He says. Nigel leans in the car, and starts the engine, It turns over. "You're a genius, my man." Nigel says with a smile.

Smiley says with a grumble, "Good. Now can we get the fuck out of here?"

Benjamin stands up and puts the ring in his pocket being careful not to let anybody see him do it. Horace walks over to him and says, "Yo, what was wrong with the car, man? This car's been giving me trouble since I got it."

"Where did you get this car?" Benjamin asks. Horace looks around for a bit then says, I bought it at an auction last year."

Benjamin looks at the car and says, "And those places never tell who the previous owner was."

"Nope." Horace says.

Benjamin takes a few steps back and says, "You need to get this car off the road. It's not safe. It'll run for now but I'm not sure for how long. Be careful on the highway. I'm not sure how fast the car will go before the engine will die. And also, don't go to fast. If you do, it'll probably conk out again."

Smiley starts to move toward Benjamin but Tom grabs him by the arm and says, "Don't do it. We're almost done. We're al—" Smiley moves his hand and moves toward Benjamin and says, "I need to be someplace fast." Ben turns to Smiley and says, "I'm not done asking questions about this car. Hold your horses." Smiley brandishes his weapon his gun and says, "You don't understand the situation." Ben takes out his own gun and proclaims, "I understand the situation perfectly. These guys taxi people all around The Bronx for cash only. They called me because they can't call a tow truck. Horace is illegal, and Nigel's on parole. You have a white man in the back seat who seems a bit nervous, and you're very anxious to be on your way. I know the make, model and license plate of this car. I could call the police right now and let them take care of it. You want that?" Smiley looks at Ben saying nothing. "I served in the Army and gun is legal and registered in my name. Is yours?" Smiley smiles slightly at Ben and starts to walk toward him. Horace comes in between them and says, "Nobody wants that. Everybody relax. It's all good. It's all good. Yo Benji. After we drop them off, we won't use this car anymore. OK?" Horace looks at Benjamin with almost desperation in his eyes.

"Please man. For your own safety." There's some real serious shit happening." Ben says to Horace. He then glances over at Smiley and whispers to Horace, "Your friend is a real asshole. He needs to watch himself."

Ben starts to back away and move toward his car. Horace starts to smile and says, "You got it, Benji. Thanks again, man. You're a lifesaver." Nigel lets the car down from the car as Smiley slowly gets back inside the car. Once in, he puts his gun away. Tom also returns to the car, turns to Smiley and asks, "Was that really necessary?"

Ben gets in his car and drives away. Nigel and Horace also get back in the car. "Who the fuck was that?" Smiley asks. "Benji is the chief engineer at Eagle Motors. He can do anything with a car. Boost it, fix it, anything." They start to drive off. "Remember, not too fast." Nigel says. "I remember." Horace snaps back.

*

The car stops on the corner of Bronx Park East and Waring Ave. "This is it?" Horace asks. Tom looks at Smiley. Smiley smiles at Horace and Nigel. Smiley takes out money and pays them. He then shows them a large wad of cash and says, "Tell me where he lives." Horace says, "I really wish I knew." Nigel smiles takes the money and says, "I do."

*

Smiley and Tom walk across the walkway overlooking the Bronx River Parkway which is where the rear entrance to the Botanical Gardens is. They get to the gate, and at the security post sits an old black man. Smiley walks over to him, smiles and says, "Kunta Kinte!" The man glares at Smiley and snaps, "My name is Tobias, not fucking Kunta!" Smiley waves him off and says, "Whatever man." Tobias looks at Tom and says, "Who's this?" Smiley looks at Tom, looks at Tobias and says, "My lawyer." He throws Tobias some money as they walk past him. "Try not to make a mess." Tobias yells at Smiley.

They walk down a path until they get to a bench. Smiley sits down. Tom stands there for a minute and sits down also. Tom stares at Smiley then looks ahead. He taps his foot and rubs his legs and stares at Smiley again. Smiley stares straight ahead and asks, "Something you want to ask me?" Tom turns in his direction and asks, "How did you know Jason was Clayton? When did you know?" Smiley looks at Tom them stares ahead and says, "I had my suspicions, but someone confirmed it for me." "Confirmed by who?" Tom asks. He stares at Smiley who ignores him. Tom takes a deep breath and says, "Fine. But at least tell me this. You were the contact the cops were looking for that night we met right? Were you the contact to Jason?"

"No. It was Gamble." Smiley says very nonchalantly. "But you shot that kid, right?" Tom asks.
Smiley turns to Tom and says, "I didn't have to. Gamble always had a short fuse; he just needed the push. He shot Angel. Once Angel was dead, I killed Gamble and Milo, grabbed the cash and split."

"So, you knew Angel was a snitch." Tom says.

"Everyone knew he was a snitch." Smiley replies back.

"So why were you there? Tom asks.

"Boozer wanted me there cause I'm good with a gun. Besides, the money was too tempting." Smiley continues. He pauses for a bit then says, "I heard the other snitch Beck was shot at point-blank range." He stares at Tom who is at first staring ahead. He finally turns to Smiley and asks, "What the fuck are you look at me like that for?"

"Cause I know you killed him, right?" Smiley asks.

Tom stands up and steps away a little and says, "None of your fucking business." Smiley smiles at him and says, "You're playing this all wrong. This whole cops and robbers dynamic is based on one concept. Perception. The way you look, dress, act, walk and talk, people make assumptions about you. You need to use this to your advantage."

Tom gets in Smiley's face and says, "Who the fuck are you to give me advice! You're nothing but a common criminal."

Smiley gets closer to him and says, "Really? You see me walking around with my pants down to my ass?" Smiley pulls his pants down to show his ass. He also slouches a bit, purses his lips and swings his arms wildly. "Ayo whatup nigga? Where you at tho? And I was like fuck dat shit nigga. Wha' happen?" Smiley then stands back up straight and says, "I am a better class of criminal. I don't talk like I have a fourth-grade education and I don't dress like I just got out of jail. I'm polite, and I always wear a belt. Most of these idiots get themselves in trouble for the stupidest reasons. If you're holding and you have to take the train, pay your fare! Most of them get caught for fare beating. If you have a gun on you, don't play loud music. Don't call attention to yourself. I rarely get stopped by the cops. And whenever I do go to the city, I put on a nice suit, carry a briefcase and I wear my glasses."

"You wear glasses?" Tom asks.

"No, they're prop glasses, but people who do wear glasses are perceived to be thirty-five percent smarter than people who don't. With the glasses, I seem even less of a threat. And I never show fear. You show fear; you get shot. Most of these wannabe thugs have never killed before. They don't know how to." Smiley says with steely determination.

Tom pauses for a bit and says, "But you've killed before."

Smiley smiles slightly and says, "The first time I killed was to protect a secret. I was eleven."

"Was it worth it?" Tom asks.

"At the time, absolutely." Smiley responds.

Tom takes a long look around then turns to Smiley and asks, "Think they'll find us?" Smiley looks back at Tom, smiles and says, "In here? Never. Do you know where they'll look? In pool halls, bars and bowling alleys. They'll never find us in a place like this."

*

Ridley and Big Ben have just walked out of a bar. Ridley has a furious and tired look on his face. Big Ben puts his hand on

Ridley and says, "Man, I told you he wouldn't in there." Ridley pushes his hand off forcefully and says, "Shut the fuck up and get your fucking hand off me, man! What about that bowling alley on Gun Hill?"

"I just spoke to Woody. He ain't there man. Smiley is fucking long gone by now." Big Ben says. Ridley stares straight ahead thinking. Big Ben takes a few toward him. He starts to put his hand on Ridley's shoulder but decides at the last minute not to do it. He says, "Look, it's late, and we're tired. I'm fucking starving, and the sun will come up soon. Let's go back to the crib and figure out our next move." Ridley turns to Big Ben and says, "Let's do that. We'll wait for the sun to come up. I think it's time shake that asshole's tree again." Ridley starts to walk away. Big Ben follows behind him and finally asks, "Which asshole are we talking about?"

"Guess." Ridley says.

*

Back at the Botanical Gardens, Tom is sitting on a bench across from Smiley who is standing. "How'd you find out about this place?" Tom asks. Smiley is looking up at the sky and trees and says, "The Botanical Gardens have been here for decades officer."

"That's not what I mean. I mean—" Tom says.

"I know what you meant." Smiley responds. He takes out an expensive looking camera, moves closer to the tree and starts to focus on a large insect on the tree. "I come here to take pictures." Smiley says as he takes a few pictures of the insect. Tom stares at him for a second then says, "You're serious." Smiley looks at the pictures he just took, turns to Tom and says,

"Of course I'm serious. You have a problem with that? Photography is my way of knowing there's more to this life than the shit we have to trudge through every day. Most people wouldn't understand it. Boozer didn't. He had a problem with it. But he was also afraid of the dark. Can you believe that? If that secret got out, he would have been killed years ago."

"You never told anybody?" Tom asks.

"No need. We found out each other's secret at the same time. Instead of turning on each other, we decided to keep our secrets to ourselves." Smiley says.

Tom stands up and takes a few steps toward Smiley and asks, "What's your secret?" Smiley looks at him and says, "Anyway, my ultimate goal is to open my own art gallery with the pictures I've been taking over the years and now that both Boozer and Clayton are dead, I finally get my chance to get out of this life. I'm not sure if you know this, but the shelf life for people in the drug trade is not very long."

Tom slightly laughs and says, "It's not very long for dirty cops either."

"I've been planning my out for years. I have my packet and my two exit strategies set." Smiley says.

"Two?" Tom asks.

"If things are cool in the city, I can just drive away, but if things get hot for me, I have someone waiting for me under the bridge. You should have an escape plan too. Just in case." Smiley says. "Why?" Tom says looking puzzled. Smiley smiles slightly and says, "A cop on the take? How long do you think you'll last? You're in bed with criminals. You might not think so now, but when Ridley finds out Clayton is dead, trust me, he will come looking for you. But remember what I said about perception. Use that to your advantage."

Smiley looks up and sees the sun is starting to come up. He picks up one of the bags of money and starts to walk away. Tom sees him do this and asks, "Where are you going?" Smiley doesn't turn back and break his stride. He says, "Don't worry about where I'm going. You can keep that other bag. I can't carry it anyway."

"What the fuck am I supposed to do now?" Tom yells as Smiley is walking further and further. "I suggest working on an exit strategy." Smiley yells back.

Tom grabs the bag and walks briskly to catch up to Smiley. He finally does and says, "Well some of can't just drop this like garbage when they want to. I hate this shit, but my wife is enjoying the life and pushing me to keep going."

"Well if you have to put that bag down, make sure it's secure and doesn't get stolen. There's a couple million in there." Smiley says.

They are outside of the park and walking in the street.

"Well, I can't take this home. If that bitch I married sees this, it'll be gone before you know it." Tom says.

"You can't leave it here, either." Smiley responds. Tom stands there and watches Smiley walk out of sight. He checks the time and walks down the street. He sees a cab coming down and puts his hand out. The cab pulls over, Tom gets in, and the car drives off.

Chapter Eight

The taxi drives to the Bedford Park section of the Bronx and stops at a bar on Jerome Avenue. Tom hands him a fifty-dollar bill. "Keep the change." Tom says. The driver turns around to Tom and says, "You want me to drop you off here? At a bar this time of morning? If you're wanting to have a drink now, that might be an issue." Tom opens the door and is halfway out of the car, and the driver yells, "Did you hear me, man? This is an issue!" Tom exits the car with his bag and sticks his head in the passenger side window and states, "This is the Bronx." He walks in the bar as the taxi drives away.

Inside, there are three old men already sitting at the bar. Behind the bar is a middle-aged man named Foley. He sees Tom walk in and is a little shocked. "Tom!" Foley says. "I've never seen you in here this early."

Tom walks further in the bar and heads to where Foley is behind the bar. "I need to drop something off here and pick it up later. Is that OK?" Tom asks.

"Of course. No problem. Just drop it off here. It'll be safe." Foley says as he allows Tom behind the bar. "You sure about that?" Tom asks. Foley moves close to Tom and says in a low, sinister tone, "You know, this is not my first rodeo with the police. Other cops have dropped shit off before. Trust me. It's safe. Can I fix you a drink?" Foley asks. Tom looks at the clock on the wall and sees its seven thirty in the morning. He looks at Foley and says with a laugh, "Nah, it's way too early."

His phone rings and Tom heads outside. He answers it without looking at who it is. "Yeah, who's this?" Tom asks with directness. "Honey? It's me." Amy says in a lovely and gentle tone. Tom's face falls, and he rolls his eyes so wide, he actually saw his brain in the back of his head. "Are you OK? I haven't seen you in days. When are you coming home? I want you to see the work that's being done on the house." Amy continues.

"I'll see it later. I have to go." Tom says as he hangs up the phone abruptly. A few seconds later, the phone rings again. Tom sucks his teeth, rolls his eyes and answers the phone saying, "I said I'd see it later."

"Clayton was shot dead last night motherfucker." Ridley says. The sound of his voice makes Tom stop in his tracks. "I heard. So?" Tom responds.

"So, I want my motherfucking money." Ridley says.

"I don't have your money." Tom responds.

"Don't fucking lie to me. Maybe I should come over to your house to see if it's there." Ridley says.

"Don't bother. I'm on my way to you right now." Tom says then hangs up and goes back inside the bar. He looks at Foley and says, "I'll take that drink now." Foley widens his eyes, grabs a glass and says, "Sure thing. Scotch. Neat?" Tom nods. Foley pours it and slides it over to Tom. He down it in one gulp. He puts the glass down and says, "I'll be back." Tom leaves the bar.

*

Tom is now standing in front of Ridley's door. He takes a deep breath, the starts pounding on it. "Ridley! Open this fucking door!" Tom yells. Lando opens to door and says, "What the fuck is wrong with you banging on the door like that this time of morning. We got neighbors!" Tom pushes Lando out of the way and makes his way to the kitchen where Ridley and Big Ben are waiting. Tom looks around and sees several guns laid out on the table. Big Ben is eating Chinese food. Pudgy is standing behind Ridley. Lando moves behind Tom. Tom looks at Ridley and says, "I fucking thought I told you not to call me again." Ridley takes out a copy of the morning paper and slams it on the table. "You read the headline?" Ridley asks. Tom looks down at the headline, and it reads, "Poetic Justice." There is a picture of Clayton/Jason's dead body on the cover.

"Congratulations. You can read. What the fuck does that have to do with me?" Tom says with steely eyes. Ridley sits back in his chair staring at Tom then says, "He had a lot of fucking money in that house, and now it's gone."

"And how do you know that? Your reliable sources? Smiley?" Tom asks.

"Where is he?" Ridley demands as he bangs on the table.

I'm sorry. Is banging on the table supposed to motivate me? Tom says sarcastically. Ridley glares at him. "And how the fuck would I know where he is?" He continues.

Ridley leans back in his chair and says, "You forget, one anonymous phone call from me and your fucking life is over. You see what happened to Russell? You want that shit? Or maybe you want that nice ass house of yours burnt to the ground."

Tom leans on the table and gets in Ridley's face and asks, "Are you threatening me motherfucker?" Big Ben laughs a bit and says, "Look who finally woke the fuck up. This white boy can't fuck with us." Tom turns to Big Ben and says, "Shut the fuck up fat man and eat another chicken wing with hot sauce." Big

Ben drops his smile and looks at Ridley who is looking very intently at Tom who is still glaring at Big Ben. Ridley then turns to Lando and says, "Hey! You frisk this asshole?" Lando briefly looks down and away from Ridley and says, "Nah, he rushed passed me. I ain't get a chance."

Ridley then turns to Tom and says, "Give him your weapon." Tom looks Ridley dead in the eye and says, "I'm not giving him shit." Ridley looks at Big Ben, and they both take their guns out and aim it at Tom. Ridley looks at Lando and says, "Take it. We got you covered." Lando slowly walks over and starts to pat Tom down. He finds Tom's service weapon and starts to remove it. "I'll take that." Lando says.

Tom reaches for the small pistol Jason gave him earlier from his ankle. "Here, take this too." Tom says and shoots Lando in the throat. Ben and Pudgy jump back at seeing this, but Ridley continues to sit there motionless. Lando holds his throat and flops around on the floor gasping for air. He moves less and less until he doesn't move at all. Big Ben yells, "Oh shit!!" Tom looks at Ridley still holding the gun and says, "Why don't you call nine one one and say you're a criminal and drug dealer and a cop shot your unarmed buddy. Can you send a unit over to check it out?" Tom then takes back the gun Lando took from him and says, "I'll take that back now."

Ridley looks over to Pudgy and says, "You want that raise? You want what Lando was getting? Shoot this motherfucker right now." Pudgy asks, "The same thing?"

"I'll fucking double it right now if you shoot him." Ridley says. Pudgy moves closer to Tom points his gun at him and says, "Talk some shit now motherfucker." Tom glances at Pudgy, Big Ben then Ridley and says, "Officer down. Ninety seconds after that call goes out, and this area will be a fucking war zone.

It will be flooded with cops, SWAT, dogs, and helicopters. They will lock this place down within a twenty-five block radius. No one gets in, and no one gets out. A thousand cops with itchy trigger fingers will kick down doors to catch a motherfucker. That means your baby mama won't get to cash that welfare check right away. She'll have to wait to get their hair did."

Ridley waves him off and says, "Whatever motherfucker. Just wait till I tell them you stole my money." Tom looks at Ridley, smiles and says, "You really think they're gonna give a fuck about that with a dead cop on the floor? They just might shoot you right there and let you bleed out and give a fuck how it'll read in the paper. I'm set to retire in a few months. I've shaken hands with every major and minor politician in this city for the last twenty-five years. I've got a list of commendations as long as my cock and please don't be mistaken that the NYPD will take your word over mine. And you think civil rights activists are going to protest your death saying how your life mattered? Cops the world over will attend my funeral and praise me for being a beacon of light in these dark times. And let me take this to the next level." Tom goes over to Big Ben who is still eating Chinese food and throws it all on the floor. Big Ben jumps back and says, "What the fuck?!"

Tom gets way in Big Ben's face and says, "Shut the fuck up you fat fucking piece of shit! For your information, I am not a white boy. I am a white man. A white man with a badge who was killed by black men with criminal records. Do you know what the public will say? Any ideas? You think they'll these black men were upstanding members of society and tried to uplift the community? No. They'll say 'when will these stupid fucking niggers learn? Those niggers got what they fucking deserved.' And they don't serve fried chicken and Chinese food in prison you fat fuck." Tom then turns to Ridley and says, "I don't know where your fucking money is? You need to talk to Smiley. If you had an ounce of brains, you would lose my number. You call me again, I'll be coming back, and I won't be alone. I'll be bringing my gang. All thirty-five thousand members. You want to fuck with that? You want to fuck with me?"

Tom then starts to grab a stack of bills lying on the table. Ridley stands up and says, "What the fuck are you doing?" Tom looks him in the eye and says, "The last time I was here, I had to kill because you wanted your money's worth. Well, I just killed again. But this time, I want my money's worth." Tom pushes past Pudgy and leaves. Big Ben, Pudgy, and Ridley sit there in silence looking at each other. Big Ben finally says, "Yo. What the fuck got into him?"

Ridley staring straight ahead says, "The cop finally got into him."

Big Ben looks at Ridley and says, "The fuck do we do now?"

In the stairwell, Tom is walking down. He stops for a moment, stares at the floor, smile broadly and continues down.

*

Tom goes back to the bar and sees a few more people are there. Foley sees him and walks over and says, "That was fast."

"I could use that drink, Foley." Tom says in a low voice.

"Sure thing." Foley responds. Foley pours him a drink which Tom downs very quickly. He then takes out a fifty-dollar bill, lays it on the bar and says, "One more for the road. Make it a double." Foley pours him a double scotch and is amazed how fast Tom drank them both.

"I've never known you to drink this much before." Foley says.

"I'm doing a lot of things I never did before." Tom says before grabbing his bag and leaving the bar.

*

The next morning, Smiley is standing across the street behind his car with a camera in his hand. The camera has a reasonably long zoom lens. After a few minutes, Benjamin walks out of his building, and Smiley starts taking pictures. Benjamin is just standing there, so Smiley continues to take a few pictures. Then Preeti comes out after him. She looks to be four or five months pregnant. Smiley takes pictures of them as they hold hands and kiss as they walk down the street together. Smiley takes pictures of the number of the building and the street the building is on. After he's finished, he smiles to himself and leaves.

Chapter Nine

In the laundromat, there are a few people folding clothes. Joanna is reading a magazine. Suddenly, a huge fist pounds on the desk. A few people in the place turn and look up. Joanna is startled and jumps. She looks up and sees Ridley, Big Ben and Pudgy. Joanna starts speaking Chinese to them. Ridley looks at her with a hard gaze as she continues to speak to them in Chinese.

Ridley grabs her by the hair and says, "Let's go bitch." Ridley and Ben lead her to the basement while Pudgy keeps watch upstairs. A few people are still looking over at what's happening. "Mind yo fucking business!" Pudgy says as he brandishes his weapon. The patrons look away and continue folding and washing their clothes.

In the basement, Emily is working on her laptop and hears the commotion and sees Ridley push her mother down the stairs. "What's going on?" Emily says to her mother. Joanna looks to the staircase and makes a slight hand signal. Emily tries to run up the ladder, but Big Ben stops her and knocks her to the floor. Big Ben takes out his gun and says, "Just say the word, man." Ridley is standing over Joanna and says, "This bitch thinks I'm fucking playing around? Shoot that bitch!" Big Ben moves toward Emily and points the gun to her head and cocks it. Joanna stands up and says, "No! Please! Don't hurt her. Do whatever you want to me but leave her alone." Big Ben and Ridley look at each other. "Shit!" Big Ben says. "I fucking knew it. I knew she spoke English." Joanna takes a small step toward Ridley and says, "What do you want?" Ridley walks around the basement area and says, "I know Boozer hid money in here. Tell me where it is."

"All the money was in his apartment. He didn't want to hide any money here. He was paranoid it would get stolen." Joanna says.

"What about the old story of all that money from the Chinese gang?" Big Ben says.

"None of it was true. It was all lies." Joanna says with tears coming down her face. "Fuck." Big Ben says.

Ridley moves toward her and says, "That's really too bad. Too bad for you." Ridley grabs Joanna by the neck.

*

Later that day at the Sims' home, Tom, Amy, and Sabrina are standing outside their house looking at all of the work done to the exterior. The roof has been retiled, and the house has a nice fresh coat of paint. Tom is wearing a very expensive black suede jacket. Standing with them is Carlos. He is a middle-aged Mexican man who is standing there with some of his men who did the job. Amy walks over to Tom and adjusts his jacket and smiles. Tom smiles slightly and looks away. "What are you getting shy for? It looks good on you." Amy says beaming. Tom holds out his arms looking at himself and says, "I know, but it's doesn't seem like me."

Carlos walks over to Tom and says, "That's a very nice jacket, Mr. Sims."

"Please, call me Tom and thank you. It's a gift from my wife." Tom responds. Amy walks in between the and says, "It's OK. He can call you Mr. Sims. It's more respectful." Tom and Carlos glance at each other. "Try not to get it dirty or wet. And please don't get any blood on it. It is suede after all."

Tom looks at Amy and says, "I'll do my best." He turns to Carlos and says, "Let me go inside and get the final payment for you guys." Tom goes into the house as Amy turns toward to Carlos and his men.

"You and your guys did a fantastic job. It was fast and neat. Really great work." Amy says.

"Thank you, ma'am." Carlos responds with a small grin.

She takes a few steps in his direction and asks, "Are all you guys from Mexico?" Carlos looks at his men briefly and says, "Uhh yes ma'am. We are."
"So, you guys are all illegals?" Amy says again.

"We're just here to do a good job and get paid fairly for our work." Carlos says back.

Amy gets very close to his face and says, "By coming into my country illegally? If you're here illegally, we don't have to give you a final payment." Carlos stands firm and says, "Begging your pardon ma'am but our status had no bearing on the quality of the work we do. We were hired because the other contractors were too expensive. You wanted a high-quality service at a low cost. If you don't pay us, that would be illegal." Amy gets very close to him and says, "Who will you call? The police? This is my country. One phone call to Immigration and Customs Enforcement, they'll deport you faster than you can spit."

Carlos gets right in her face and says, "Call them. Do you know what they'll find? We are all US Citizens. We were all born here. Our parents were born here. Our grandparents came here in search of a better life. Do you know who else is a US

Citizen? My cousin who also happens to be a producer for the Spanish news network. They will report how a police officer and his wife paid cash for work that exceeds their income. They will wonder how he was able to afford to pay for all of this work. They will investigate. Then you will be deported. To a jail cell."

Amy steps back with her eyes wide and mouth slightly open. "Wait. All of you guys are citizens? How is that possible?" She asks.

"Your husband made sure we were all legal because he knew you would threaten to deport us." Carlos says to her with a smile. She turns to his men who are all smiling at her. A few of them give her a thumbs up. One of his men gives Amy a broad smile and says, "Make America Great Again."

Tom comes outside with an envelope and hands it to Carlos. "Here you go. There's a little extra in there because you guys met your deadline." He says giving Carlos a very firm handshake. "Thank you very much."

One of the workers whispers, "¿Cómo puede un hombre tan bueno estar casado con una mujer tan horrible?" Amy walks over the workers and says, "What did he say? Speak English!" Tom give Amy a very sarcastic look and shake each member of Carlos' team and says, "Gracias chicos por todo vuestro arduo trabajo." They all look shocked at Tom. He smiles and enters the house. As Carlos and his men leave, Amy and Sabrina follow Tom inside.

Inside the house, Tom is standing in the living room in amazement. "This place looks great! I mean it looks like a brand new house!" Sabrina walks in front of him and says, "I sent you pictures of the updates."

"Yeah, I know. I've been kind of busy." Tom says putting his head down. Sabrina takes a step closer to him and says, "I know. Where have you been? It's been since forever when I saw you last. What are you doing out there?" Amy steps in front of Sabrina and says, "I told you before never to ask your father his business." Sabrina takes a step back from her mother and says, "But he promised to teach me how to drive." Tom moves closer to his daughter and put his hands on her shoulders and says, "I know. And I promise I will. I'll be spending more time at home now. I'll teach you how to drive and once you get your license, I'll buy you a new car."

Sabrina looks up at her father and says, "Really??"

"Really." Tom replies back. Sabrina throws her arms around Tom. She starts kissing him all over his face. Tom pulls Amy and Sabrina close to him and says, "I want to show you guys something, but you have to promise not to tell anyone. I mean anyone. Not Debbie, not any friends at school, no one. Understand?"

"Yes, daddy." Sabrina says.

"Yes, daddy." Amy says.

Tom starts to go upstairs when there is loud banging on his front door. The banging frightens Sabrina and Amy. Tom takes out his gun from his ankle holster and moves toward the door. He motions for Amy and Sabrina to step away which they do together. Tom puts his hand on the doorknob, takes a deep breath and opens the door to find Carlos standing with a worried look on his face. As soon as Carlos sees the gun, he puts his hands up and says, "I'm sorry about this, but there is a woman out here screaming your name." Tom comes outside a little lowering his weapon. "What woman?" Tom asks. Carlos points down the street. Tom looks in that direction and sees Joanna walking towards him. She is badly beaten and bloody walking very carefully towards the house. Her top is almost completely ripped off, and she has cuts and bruises all over her and a black eye.

"Fuck!" Tom yells as he puts his gun away and runs towards Joann. He rips off his suede jacket and puts it around her shaking body and leads her in the house.

 "Who's she?" Sabrina asks.

"What the hell is going on?" Amy asks. Tom looks at Sabrina and says, "Sabrina, get her a glass of water and get my phone." Sabrina stands there motionless and says, "But who is she?"

Tom stops, turns to Sabrina and yells, "Will you get her a fucking glass of fucking water and fetch my fucking cell phone?? Do it! Now!! Sabrina runs into the kitchen as Tom sits Joanna down on the couch. He bends down in front of her and says in a soft voice, "Who did this?" Joanna is looking down at the floor, and her body is still shaking, but she slowly looks up in Tom's face and says, "Ridley. He and his gang did this to me." Sabrina hands her the water which she drinks most of. Tom walks over to the kitchen and grabs some towels and wets them. He bends over to Joanna and reaches for her face. She pulls back a little.

"It's OK. You're safe here. I won't hurt you." Tom says. Joanna nods slightly, and Tom gently cleans her face. Amy sees this and says, "Oh, don't use the good towels. I just bought those. Use the old ones from the linen closet." Tom stands up very quickly and glares at her with a look of contempt and disgust. Amy wisely backs away a little. He looks at Sabrina and motions at his phone. She hands him his phone and starts to dial as Joanna drinks more water. "Who are you calling?" Amy asks. "We have to get her to a hospital." Tom says. Joanna drops the glass of water on the floor and slaps the phone out of Tom's hand. Amy looks very annoyed at the broken glass and water all over her just redone floors.

Tom jumps back a little and says, "What the hell?" Joanna starts to pulls at Tom's clothes and says, "No! No hospitals. They will kill her." Tom grabs her wrists and says, "Wait! Stop! Kill who? Who will they kill?"

"My daughter. They will call every hospital in the area every hour, and if they hear my name, they will kill her." Joanna says through tears in her eyes. Tom stands there for a minute trying to figure out what to do next. "Fuck." Tom says.

"What do we do? She needs a hospital." Amy says.
"Or at the very least, a doctor." Sabrina says. Tom looks over to Sabrina, raises his eyebrows and snaps his fingers. "That's it!" He exclaims. He grabs his wallet and starts searching desperately. Every card that is not what he's looking for; he lets it fall to the floor.

"What the fuck are you looking for?" Amy asks. He finally finds the card he was looking for. "Sabrina, take her upstairs to the guest bedroom." Tom says. Sabrina helps Joanna stand up and leads her up the stairs. Joanna turns around and asks, "Who are you calling?"

Tom looks up at her and says, "A doctor." Tom watches them go up the stairs and as soon as they are out of his sight, he dials the number. "Hello, doctor? This is Officer Sims? Tom Sims? We met the night you patched up Smiley?"

"Yes, how can I help you?" The doctor responds.

"I have an emergency. I need you over here at my house right away." Tom says with urgency.

There is a slight pause then the doctor says, "Give me your address."

*

Sometime later, Tom opens his front door the lets the doctor in. He his carrying a backpack with him. "Where is she?" he asks. "I put her in the upstairs bedroom. This way." Tom says and leads him to where Joanna is. The doctor goes inside while Tom goes back downstairs.

Tom is sitting in a chair shaking his leg and biting his nails when the doctor comes back downstairs. Tom stands up to meet him. "So? How is she?" Tom asks. The doctor moves closer to Tom and says in a low voice, "She's in shock. She was also gang raped and badly beaten." "She didn't want to go to the hospital. She actually said she couldn't go to the hospital."

"Well, rape victims get lots of attention. Especially police attention." The doctor says. Tom looks up at the ceiling and says, "Can I see her?" The doctor looks at Tom then looks at the ceiling and says, "Keep it brief. I gave her something to relax her but it's not working. She very agitated."

In the bedroom, Joanna is sitting in a chair staring at the wall. There is a slight knock on the door, and Tom slowly walks in. He closes the door behind him and carefully walks over to Joanna. He kneels down next to her. He takes her hand, but she pulls her hand away. "I need to know exactly what Ridley told you. Please tell me. I want to help you. I want to help your daughter. What did he tell you?"

Joanna is still staring at the wall then turns to Tom and says, "He told me if he doesn't get the money from you and Smiley tonight, he'll kill Emily. He wants Smiley to deliver the money alone to his place before midnight. If he even thinks you're nearby, he will kill her." Tom slowly stands up and says, "But I don't even know where Smiley is." Joanna is now crying and says, "You have to help me! Please! You just have to. I told Ridley you would help me for the same reason he said you wouldn't."

"What reason is that?" Tom asks.

"Because you're a cop." Joanna says. Tom slowly walks out of the room and shuts the door behind him. He takes out his badge and stares at it as tears start to come down his face.

Tom is now standing in the backyard motionless. A few minutes later the doctor joins him. He sees the doctor and says, "What the fuck am I going to do? How am I going to get this girl back?" The doctor says, "She has faith in this city and the police."

"No. She has faith in me!!" Tom yells as he bangs in chest. "She is relying on me to bring her daughter back in one piece. How the fuck am I going to do that? How can I get Smiley back? I have no clue where he is or how to contact him." He continues.

The doctor looks up at him and says, "I can call him." Tom looks shocked and asks, "You do?? How?"

"I have his number." The doctor says.

"What??" Tom says confused.

"I have all of their numbers. I make house calls, remember?"
The doctor says. Tom gives a half laugh and says, "Give me
your phone." The doctor hands him his phone and says,
"You're going to call him now? He's probably gone by now."

Tom walks around his backyard wagging his finger and says,
"No. I saw him last night. It'll take him a while to find an exit.
He's not out yet but will be soon." The doctor moves near him
and says, "What are you going to do to get him here? You
know him by now. He's tough."

Tom smiles slightly and says, "Go check on Joanna. I'll get him
here." The doctor goes back to the house leaving Tom alone
with his thoughts.

Chapter Ten

Smiley is in the waiting room of a rental car office in Manhattan wearing a very professional dark grey suit, crisp white shirt, and a matching tie. He is also wearing Oxford shoes, glasses and reading a copy of the New York Times. Sitting next to him are two huge suitcases. After sitting there for a few minutes, his phone rings and he sees it's from the doctor.

"What's up, doc?" Smiley says. "Travis." Tom says on the phone. Smiley pauses for a minute and then says, "Tom?" He gets up and walks out of the office. He covers the phone with his hand and barks, "What the fuck do you want? Why are you calling me?"

"We have a problem. Ridley found out what happened to Jason. He beat the shit out of Joanna, raped her and is holding Emily hostage. If he doesn't get the money by tonight, he'll kill her." Tom says. "Sounds like a job for the NYPD or SWAT. Maybe both." Smiley responds.

"I can't call them for backup. For one, it would be too hard to explain. And two, Ridley wants you to deliver the money personally. Where are you?" Tom asks.

"None of your fucking business." Smiley says. At that moment, a handsome young man named Carlton comes out of the office and taps Smiley on the shoulder and says, "Excuse me. Mr. Marvin? I'm so sorry for the delay, but the car you requested just became available. I know you initially ordered an Eagle, but we've been getting complaints about those cars so—"

Smiley covers the phone with his hand. "No. No. No! I don't want Eagle. I need a reliable car for travel. My business needs me. This is them on the phone now. Did you get the new car?" Smiley asks. "We did. It took us some time to prepare it for you. Just give us a few more minutes, and we'll bring it around thirty-ninth street." Carlton says.

"Four-door and a huge trunk?" Smiley says. "Absolutely. We also had to kind of scramble because you called us with little warning. I hope this doesn't delay your business." Carlton says.

"Neither do I." Smiley says and watches Carlton go back inside. He gets back on the phone with Tom and says, "Look,--"

"That makes sense how you plan on getting out of the city. With that money, you can't fly, and a train is too risky. You probably had these false documents made years ago. If you're in midtown after rush hour, it will probably take you about thirty minutes to get back here." Tom says.

"What the fuck can you do to stop me?" Smiley asks.

"Easy. I'll tell the police to be on the lookout for a black male between the ages of thirty-five and forty-five about six feet tall and a hundred and seventy-five to one hundred eighty pounds. He will be wearing a very sharp suit, glasses and will look most likely very unassuming." Tom says.

"And why would the cops look for me? Why would they want to stop me?" Smiley asks with a raised voice.

"The murder of two people last night in the Bronx. One of them was a former police officer." Tom says.

Smiley looks around him then uses his other hand to cover the phone and says, "A fucking corrupt police officer. Murders you witnessed."

"And how are you going to explain all of that money on you? You'll have a lot of explaining to do." Tom says.

The veins in Smiley's neck and heads are now bulging. He says, "Let me ask you a question, motherfucker. What do you think is going to happen when this goes to trial? What do you think I'll say? You're not thinking ahead."

"No motherfucker. You're not thinking ahead. You think Ridley will let you live long enough to see a trial. Once you're in the lockup, I'll make sure Ridley knows where you are. You'll be dead in less than twenty-four hours." Tom says.

"So will the girl." Smiley.

"You now have twenty-seven minutes to get to my house." Tom says. A large sedan is brought out in front of Smiley. Carlton gets out of the car and hands Smiley the keys. "You are all ready to go Mr. Marvin. Again, I apologize for the delay. We've taken the liberty of loading your bags in the trunk. Smiley gets in the car and holds the phone to his ear.

"If your ass is not at my house in twenty-seven minutes, your face will be all over the news, and this city will be shut down. You won't make two blocks in midtown. You will be caught. You will go to jail, and you will be killed. Do you think I'm fucking around? Try me." Tom says before he hangs up. Smiley sits there for a minute then pulls on the steering wheel and says, "Fuck! Fuck! Fuck!" Carlton sees Smiley yelling and screaming from inside the rental office. He turns to a colleague says, "I wonder what kind of business he's in."

Tom is now sitting at his kitchen table looking at an open bag of money. He looks around his house and sees all of the work that has been done and paid for with the money. Every few minutes, he is checking the time. Amy walks in and sits next to him. "I just got off the phone with Debbie. Russell's been acting erratically lately, so they put him on suicide watch. Are you ok?" she asks. She touches his hand, and he pushes it away. "No. I'm pretty fucking far from being ok. They are going to kill this girl, and I'm afraid there's nothing I can do to stop it. There has to be a way to get this kid back."

Amy looks at him for a minute, then says, "It's very admirable that you to want to try and help her. I think you somehow feel responsible for what happened to her. But there's no way you'll be able to do this by yourself. Maybe you need to take a step back and let the rest of the force handle this from here on out." Tom turns to her and gives her a look of utter disbelief. She sees this look and says, "Please don't look at me like that. I'm serious. With this money, we can all make a fresh start. After you retire, you can take the academy job, or we can travel like we always talked about. We could move to Long Island or anywhere. It doesn't matter just as long as we are safe and together."

Tom turns to her and states, "But they will kill this girl! Don't you get it? She had nothing to do with any of this. She is completely innocent. If she dies as a result of something I did, that's on me. I have to try and save her. If I don't, I'll have to live with that guilt for the rest of my life. Did you see the look in Joanna's eyes when she asked me for help? That look is the reason why I became a cop in the first place. To protect the innocent." Amy stands up and asks, "How can you be so selfish?" Tom squints his eyes and shakes his head in disbelief and says, "Excuse me? I'm being selfish? So you don't have a problem with walking away and letting an innocent girl die?" Amy looks at him, then looks away for a bit then looks back at him and says, "Well, better her than you."

"Wow. You were right. She is a bitch." Smiley says. Tom and Amy look in the direction where Smiley is standing. Tom lets out a sigh of relief seeing Smiley. Smiley walks a little further in the house and asks, "Is this the garbage you're trying to break free from?" Amy starts breathing very heavy and asks, "What the fuck is he talking about?" Tom looks away and says, "Nothing. He's not saying anything."

Smiley turns to Amy and says, "He doesn't want to do this kind of thing anymore but feels trapped in this life because you're such a bitch. That's probably why he hasn't been spending that much time at home." Amy now turns to Tom with wide eyes and asks, "You said that?"

"I have no reason to lie." Smiley remarks. Amy now looks at Tom, and her eyes are getting watery, and she sniffs a few times. A tear falls down a face, and she asks, "Y-You said that?"

Tom grabs Smiley by the arm and leads him to the backyard and the setting sun. He gets right in Smiley's face and says, "Why don't you shut the fuck up about her? Smiley pushes him a little and yells, "Or what? The fuck are you going to do to me? I'm here, aren't I? Tom pushes him right back and says, "Did you forget what I said over the phone?" Smiley flares his nostrils, narrows his eyes and pushes Tom so hard he almost falls over. "You're not the first cop to take a bribe from me." Smiley says in a loud booming voice. Tom looks around nervously and says, "Keep your fucking voice down."

Smiley looks at Tom, smiles a little and adds, "What are you ashamed of? You weren't embarrassed when you asked for the money or when you took it? Right?" Smiley takes out a gun and points it at Tom in a very threatening way and declares, "I don't give a fuck if you're a cop or not. Show me how hard you are."

Tom sees the gun, slowly stands up and backs away while raising his hands a little. "I don't want to do this right now." Tom says.

Smiley's eyes get wide and asks, "Oh, you want to do this old school??" Smiley puts his gun away and takes off his suit jacket and goes into a fighting stance. "I will kick your ass up and down this fucking street. Let's go!" Smiley screams at him.

"I told you I don't want to do this right now." Tom says in a more calming tone.

"You can't do this right now." Smiley says. "You're Tom Sims. A twenty-four-year vet and multiple award winner. You're a fucking boy scout and have no idea what you're doing. You're improvising." Tom takes a small step toward Smiley and says, "Ridley took Emily. Look. We need to save her. I—I need to save her. That's all I care about."

Smiley takes a long look at Tom, smiles slightly and asserts, "There was a snowball effect after you took the money from me that night. At first, you liked it. You took a bite off the streets and enjoyed the taste. You were able to live well and enjoy. But then the streets started to bite back. First with Russell, then with Jason and now with this girl. You got lost in these mean streets, and now you are desperate to find your way back. You think if you save this girl you can also save yourself. To assuage your guilt and somehow redeem your humanity if you save her life. Am I right?"

Tom looks at Smiley and feels his eyes getting watery. He says in a low voice, "Yes. But I can't do this alone. I—I need you. Please."

"It's a wonderful thing that you have a goal in life. Albeit a difficult one. My goals are much simpler and easier to obtain."

Tom's shoulders fall, and he lowers his head. "You can keep the money. I don't give a fuck about that anymore."

"You can't give him the money." Amy says. They both turn around and see her standing in the doorway to the backyard. Tom turns around to face her and says, "Saving the girl is all that matters." Smiley also turns around but has a smirk on his face.

"What about me? What about your daughter? What about your family?" Amy asks. Tom stares at for a few seconds, then turns to Smiley and says, "Let's go inside and figure out a way to get this girl back." Tom goes into the house. Smiley starts to follow, but Amy blocks his path.

"Excuse me." Smiley says.

Amy uses her whole body to stand in the doorway and folds her arms. "Excuse me, what?" she says with an arrogant tone and slightly pausing in between the words 'me' and 'what'.

"Excuse me, bitch." Smiley responds back also slightly pausing in between the words 'me' and 'bitch.'

"You fucking piece of monkey shit." Amy snarls. Smiley drops his smile and glares at her. "You hear me, nigger?" Amy delivers in a low but stern voice.

Smiley looks at her up and down, gets very close to Amy's face, slightly smiles and says, "I am a criminal. I rob, steal and kill without hesitation. I'm also wearing a fifteen-hundred-dollar suit, and you'll never see me coming. I am a nigger. But I'm an upper-class nigger. The kind of nigger reserved for athletes and actors. You are the wife of one of the most decorated cops in New York City history. And you're only interested in him breaking the law. Why? Because you are a self-absorbed, ill-mannered, overweight, uneducated, poorly dressed White woman living in America. You could use a good cock in the ass but I can't you there. And people can smell your fat, dirty, cheesy, busted out cunt a fucking mile away." Amy looks at him up and down with her mouth wide open and her eyebrows raised. After a few seconds, she frowns, turns to Tom and demands, "Are you going to let him talk to me like that?" Tom stares at her saying nothing. Amy gasps a little at his silence. "You have nothing to say??" She yells at Tom.

"The fuck is he going to say?" Smiley yells to Amy. "What the fuck is he going to do? I'm here! I'm helping him, and everybody gets what they want. He gets to save the girl, I get to keep the money, and you get the fuck out of my way."

Amy smacks him in the face. Smiley's head moves to the left a little. He looks at the smug look on Amy's face and smiles before slapping her right back. Amy steps back for a second before regaining her footing. She now makes a fist and raises it like she's going to punch him. Smiley sees this, takes a step back and reaches for his gun. Tom stands in front of Amy and says, "I wouldn't do that if I were you. Smiley doesn't hesitate." She stands in front of Tom and shouts while pointing at Smiley, "He hit me! Shoot him!!"

"In this defense, you hit him first. I would have to arrest you for assault." Tom responds. He then turns to Smiley and says, "Let's go. It's getting dark and time is wasting." Smiley give Amy an enormous smile and brushes past her and bumps her shoulder in the process. Amy stands there not sure of what to do or say.

*

In the living room, Smiley and Tom are sitting across from each other. Smiley says, "The front door opens up to the living room. To the left is the kitchen."

"Ridley is always in there." Tom responds back.

"So is Big Ben's fat ass." Smiley says.

"Once you drop off the money, you have to stall them somehow until I get there." Tom says.

"And how the fuck am I supposed to do that?" Smiley asks.

Joanna slowly comes down the stairs. The doctor is following close behind. Tom gets up and helps her down the rest of the stairs. He sits her down on the couch. Tom takes a good look at her face and sees how fresh her cuts and bruises are. "How do you feel? Did you get any rest?" Tom asks. "I can't rest knowing they have my Emily." Joanna asks. She turns to Smiley and says, "Smiley."

"Joanna." Smiley says back.

"I'm surprised a fucking piece of shit like you is here to help to get my daughter back." She snarls at Smiley. Everyone stops and looks at Joanna. Smiley points to Tom and replies, "He's paying me." She winces in pain. "I have her on some heavy-duty pain meds. It has certain side effects. Looks like they're wearing off." The doctor says as he goes in his bag and hands her another pill. Joanna swallows it without water. "You guys figure out how to get her back?" Joanna asks. Her phone rings. She answers it and immediately begins to speak Chinese. She starts to yell and get very animated then hangs up in a huff.

"Once the shooting starts, we have to kill everyone." Smiley says. "OK." Tom replies back. Smiley sits on the edge of his seat, looks Tom dead in the eye and says, "You're not understanding me. I mean everyone. Everyone. The moment you walk in that apartment, you won't be a cop. We can't afford to let anyone live." Tom looks at Smiley and nods knowingly.

"Get her. Do whatever the fuck you have to do." Joanna says. Tom turns to Joanna confused and says, "Who were you talking to before?"

"Just my crazy cousin Lee. He heard what happened and wants to do something." Joanna says almost dismissively. Smiley looks up quickly and asks, "The one who owns the laundromat and the Chinese restaurant?"

"Yeah, why?" Joanna says a little confused. Tom and Smiley look up at each other. Tom smiles a little. "Call him back." Tom says. "Why? What's going on? What are we planning?" Joanna says. Smiley looks at Joanna and says, "We'll tell you on the way."

Tom stands up and says, "What do you mean 'we'? You're not going."

"She should. The more, the merrier." Smiley says as he gets up. "I'm serious. This is going to be way too dangerous for you. Especially after what happened to you earlier." Tom says.

Joanna stands up and walks over to Tom and says, "No offense, officer but you have no fucking idea who I am. I'm Asian. Back in my day, when I was running the streets, I did more drugs and fucked more guys and did shit that you wouldn't believe. I gave it all up after I had Emily because I wanted her to be innocent. And she is. Those motherfuckers have her. I will do whatever and kills whoever I have to to get her back. If you don't want to go then stay here. Smiley, my cousin and I will handle it. I'm fucking going. Do you understand?" Tom looks at Joanna and says, "Let's go." The doctor and stands up and asks in a loud voice. "Uhh before the three of you go off on a suicide mission, can I get paid for services rendered? Tom gets up, goes to his black duffel bag and throws a few stacks of money on the couch near him. "Thank you. Good night and good luck." The doctor says.

They all get up to leave the house. Sabrina walks in just as everyone is going. Joanna and Smiley walk past her. Tom stops in front of Sabrina. Amy walks over to Sabrina and puts her arms around her. Mother and daughter hold each other looking at Tom. He opens his mouth but can't form the words. Tom leaves.

After a few moments, Sabrina asks, "What's going on now?" Amy says nothing at first. Then she turns to her daughter and says, "I think I need to get out of the house. How would you like a driving lesson?"

Sabrina's face lights up with a broad smile. "Seriously! Right now?" She asks. "Right now." Amy replies. "Let's go."

Chapter Eleven

Later that night, Amy and Sabrina are in the car. Sabrina is driving, and Amy is riding shotgun. The car is moving down the street at a decent pace. Sabrina is holding the wheel appropriately while Amy is carefully watching the road and her daughter. As they are coming to an intersection, the light changes from green to yellow to red. Sabrina doesn't come to a complete stop in time and blocks the crosswalk. Amy looks out of the window on both sides and says, "You see what you just did? You're blocking the crosswalk. If you did that in the city, you would get a ticket for blocking the box and have points taken off your license. You need to back up now." Sabrina backs up until she is clear of the intersection and they wait for the light to change. "But overall you're doing good. Better than I expected."

"Well, you've been a pretty good teacher." Sabrina confesses. Amy leans over to her and says, "Actually, your father would have been much better at this than me. He's an excellent driver. He can do figure eights, drifts and other wild things."

"Really?" Sabrina says with enthusiasm as her eyes get wide. "Don't get any ideas, young lady." Amy says as they both laugh. Sabrina looks around and says, "Dad said this car has a lot of horsepower. Let me floor it until we get to the next light. Please?"

"Absolutely not. It's too dangerous." Amy says very sternly. "Please. There's no one around. Look." Amy looks all around and sees very few people. She looks ahead and sees the next light is only a quarter mile ahead. "Just this once." Amy relents. Sabrina flashes a huge smile and revs the engine very loudly. A woman in her early sixties is crossing the street, and instead of crossing at the crosswalk, she crosses behind their car. The light changes to green, and since Sabrina forgot to put the car back in drive, the car goes backward very fast and hits the woman head-on. Sabrina slams on the brakes. "What was that??" She asks nervously. Amy looks in her rear-view mirror and sees a body lying in the street. "Fuck!" She yells. She sticks her head out of the window and sees the body in the street. She looks at Sabrina breathing very heavy with her eyes very wide. "Did I just hit someone??" Sabrina says with her eyes getting watery.

"Shut up." Amy says looking around. "Oh God. I fucking killed someone. My life is fucking over!" Sabrina says now openly crying.

"I said shut up!!" Amy yells at her. "I need to think. Let's get the fuck out of here before anyone notices." Amy says.

"Umm OK. Good idea." Sabrina says. "Is the car in drive this time?" Amy asks. Sabrina puts the car in drive and says, "It is now."

"Good. Now let's wait for the light to change again and slowly move away from this area." Amy says. Sabrina sees people starting to gather around and look at the body in the street. She starts to hyperventilate and panic. Sabrina hits the gas and runs the red light in the process. She continues to speed until she gets to the next intersection. Sabrina looks ahead and goes faster. Cars coming from through that intersection have to stop short to avoid getting in an accident. "Fuck!!" Amy yells. "What the fuck do we do now??" Sabrina pleads. Amy takes out her phone and starts to dial a number. The phone rings and keeps ringing. "Fuck! Answer the fucking phone!!" Amy says.

*

Tom, Smiley, and Joanna are walking down the street. Smiley is carrying a large duffle bag when Tom's phone rings. He looks at it and sees it's his wife. He rolls his eyes and sucks his teeth and barks, "Oh Amy, leave me the fuck alone!" Smiley looks at Tom and remarks, "Why don't you shoot that bitch? Cheaper than a divorce with Ivan & Duke."

"I told you to mind your fucking business about her. Didn't I?" Tom yells. They all stop in front of the building where Ridley and his gang are and where Emily is being held captive. Tom steps in front of Smiley a little and says, "Remember, try to stall them for at least five minutes or more to give us time to get there."

Smiley looks at Tom and says, "Don't worry. I'll probably be dead in two, but I will do my best." He then turns to Joanna and asks, "What will he most likely be carrying?"

"He likes to use the double barrel shotgun for close encounters. You'll know it when you hear it. The sound is unmistakable." Joanna replies.

"I'll look out for it." Smiley says to Joanna. He turns to Tom who is already looking at him. The two men stare at each other for a minute or so saying nothing. Smiley walks to the front of the building and starts to go in. Before he does, he stops, turns to Tom and says, "So this is what it feels like."

"What?" Tom asks.

"Fear." Smiley says. He smiles slightly and enters the building.

*

Smiley slowly walks up the stairs until he gets to Ridley's door. He takes a deep breath, smiles then knocks firmly on it. Woody opens it. He has a very concerned look on his face. Behind Woody is Mookie, a black man in his twenties and ET another black man in his upper teens. Mookie and ET both have their guns drawn on Smiley. Smiley looks at Woody and says, "What are you doing here?" as he enters the apartment with his arms slightly raised. Mookie looks at Smiley up and down and says, "Nice suit nigga. Who the fuck is you supposed to be?"

Smiley turns to him and replies, "A white-collar criminal." "Keep your motherfucking hands up." Mookie says as ET comes over to pat him down. "We found him in your apartment. Searching." ET says. "Searching for what?" Smiley asks as he looks at Woody who avoids eye contact. "Fuck do I know." ET barks back.

Percival walks in from the kitchen still limping slightly. "He's clean." ET says.

Percival walks over to Smiley and asks, "Is he clean. Did you pat him down good?" Percival roughly throws Smiley up against the wall and frisks him hard. "You learn that from the police?" Smiley asks. As Percival is frisking Smiley, he gets a little too close to his private area. Smiley smiles and says, "Listen, if you want to see what I have down there, I can take you in the back and show your ass. Literally."

ET and Mookie start laughing.

"Yo, He called you a faggot, man." Mookie says.

"He said you take it in the ass." ET asks.

Percival takes out his gun and knocks Mookie upside the head knocking him down. He points the gun directly to ET's eye and yells, "You think I'm a faggot now? I'm asking you a fucking question! Do you?" Mookie and ET have both dropped their smile and look very scared. "Nah, man. I was just joking." ET says.

"Do I look like I'm fucking joking? Do I?" Percival says very menacingly.

ET raises his hands and lowers his head a little and says, "Nah man. Yo, chill the fuck out."

Mookie follows ET's lead and also raises his hands and lowers his head a little and says, "I ain't mean no disrespect. I was kidding man."

Percival takes a step towards them and says, "Don't fucking joke like that with me. You don't fucking know me! You just got here, and you're gonna try and do me like that? You fucking crazy? Rule number one, be careful with that. You say shit like that to the wrong person; you be dead like a motherfucker. You got me?"

"Yes sir." ET says.
"Y-yes sir Mr. Percival sir." Mookie says. "I need this job. I can't afford to lose this. I'm in a fucked up situation at home, you know?" he continues. Percival looks at him and says, "Join the fucking club. Let's go." He turns to Smiley and says, "Pick up that bag and follow me." Smiley picks up the bag and Percival leads them to the kitchen.

Ridley and Big Ben are sitting at the table. Several guns are laying on top of it. Everyone is just standing there as Percival waits for Ridley to say something. "You check him?" Ridley asks Percival. Percival smiles slightly at Smiley, then turns to Ridley and says, "He's clean." Ridley looks up at Percival asks, "What about the bag. You check that?" Percival drops his smile and now looks a little flushed in the face. He looks at Smiley who winks a bit at him. Ridley gets up, moves everyone out of the way and opens the bag to see it filled with money. He sticks his hand deep in the bag and pulls out a huge gun. He shows this gun to Percival, Mookie, and ET.

"Smiley has a reputation on these streets. Don't trust him." Percival says. "Where's the girl?" Smiley asks. "She still alive?"

Ridley looks at Smiley up and down and says, "What happened to Boozer? Why the fuck was he running? I thought he wasn't supposed to do anything stressful."

"Everything we do on these streets is stressful. Why do you care?" Smiley asks. "Humor me. Tell me why a man like that would kill himself? What was he running for?" Ridley says.

Smiley looks at Ridley for a bit then says, "I don't think he was running for as much as he was running from." Ridley and Big Ben glance over at each other. "Running from what?" Ridley says.

"I think he wanted out of this life. He was burnt out and tired and just looking for a way out." Smiley says. Big Ben nudges Ridley and says, "Well, he fucking found it, didn't he?" He and Ridley have a big laugh. Smiley stares at them while ET and Mookie stand still not sure what to do or say.

"Well, at least he went out on his own terms." Smiley says. Most of us don't get that option. The three of us has been doing this almost the same amount of time. We've all been shot and shot at. We've made a shit ton of enemies. Do you know how you'll end?" Smiley continues. The smiles from Ridley and Big Ben melt away. "Probably why who both spend so much time in here. And when you do go out, it's with an entourage that you use for either protection or as human shields." He continues while glaring at them. Ridley and Big Ben look at each other slightly before looking away. Big Ben waves at Smiley and says, "Whatever, man," Percival takes out his gun and points it at Smiley. "Not so tough now, right motherfucker?" He asks. Smiley looks at him and smiles. Slightly at first, then broader as the seconds pass. Percival grits his teeth and asks, "What the fuck are you smiling at?"

Smiley takes a step toward Percival and says, "You. You forget I've seen the real you. When you tried to kill me before, I had you begging for your life. I don't know your story, but you don't belong here. You want to feel tough, but deep down, you're not. When Ridley, Big Ben myself and even Boozer were cutting our teeth and making a name for ourselves on the streets, you were home waiting for your Pussy Ass Nigger membership card to come in the mail. I bet you've never killed before. Am I right? You have no idea what's it like to take a life."

"Oh yeah? Watch this." Percival says as he cocks the gun and presses it against Smiley's forehead. Smiley smiles then Big Ben stands up and says, "Whoa! Wait a minute! Not in the kitchen. That's not sanitary." He puts his hand on Percival's arm and gets him to lower the gun. Ridley stands up and says, "I need to know how much money is in that bag." He turns to Woody and says, "You and Smiley go in the back and start counting."

Smiley and Woody head to the back bedrooms when there are loud bangs on the door. They all get a little nervous except

Smiley who looks almost relieved. "Who the fuck is that?" Big Ben asks. Ridley slowly looks through the peephole and sees Lee, Joanna's cousin dressed as a short order cook with several large bags of Chinese food. Lee says in a thunderous voice and a thick, exaggerated Chinese accent, "Delivery!" Ridley turns to Big Ben and asks, "You ordered Chinese food?"

"Nah, but let's see what he got!" Big Ben says with a smile. He moves closer to the door and says, "Yo! You got wings?"

"I have four order Chicken wings. Extra hot sauce." Lee continues. "Nice! Yeah, hang on a minute. Let me get some money." Ben says as he leans toward Ridley and whispers, "Hand me that gun right there."

Ridley puts his hand on the gun and says, "But it ain't loaded." Big Ben smiles and says, "That don't matter. He don't know that. You wanna see a ching chow shit his pants? This is gonna be some funny ass shit." Ridley grabs Percival by the arm and says, "Smiley's right. It's time for you to lose that cherry. I'm giving you three minutes. If I don't hear two gunshots in three minutes, I'm sending Big Ben back there, and then I'll hear three. You understand?" Big Ben drops his smile and looks at Percival in all seriousness.

Percival takes out his gun and says, "I got this." Lee bangs on the door loudly again. "You pay now pease." Big Ben turns to the door and says, "Hold the fuck on. I'm coming." Percival walks toward the bedrooms.

As soon as Smiley is in one of the bedrooms, he drops the bag and unzips his pants where he pulls out a small switchblade that was taped to his upper inner thigh. Woody looks at him up and down with a very suspicious glare. "We don't have much time." Smiley says as turns toward the door and listens intently. "Tell me about it. You cleaned out Boozer's place, and you were going to leave town without me, right? Y-You weren't even going to say goodbye? Or even call? You were going to leave me in all this shit?" Woody asks. Smiley faces Woody and sees his eyes are tearing up. "Oh, honey." Smiley goes to kiss him and at first Woody resists but then they start kissing more passionately.

Percival is walking down the hallway to one of the bedrooms when he stops. He turns around and sees no one is behind him. Percival then starts to breathe very heavy as he leans against the wall to keep himself from falling over. His body begins to shake a little as he wipes the sweat from his hands and forehead. Percival grabs his chest and tries to catch his breath. "What--" He stutters. He checks his watch and throws his head back. "OK. Here we go." He whispers to himself. He goes to a bedroom and opens the door to see Emily gagged and tied to the chair. "Oh! Sorry!" He starts to close the door and doesn't understand the profanities she is yelling at him. He stands in front of the entrance to the second bedroom. He puts one hand on the knob and readies his other hand with the gun. He takes a deep breath and slowly opens the door and sees Smiley and Woody kissing and touching each other intimately. Percival jumps back a little not expecting to see this. Seeing them like this causes Percival to lower his gun. He smiles slightly to himself. That smile fades away to shame and anger, and his frowns his brow and clenches his teeth.
He raises his gun at them and yells, "What the fuck is you two niggers doing??"

Big Ben has his hand on the front door and says "Ready? On the count of three. One.."

In the bedroom, Percival cocks the gun and says," You faggot ass."

"Two." Big Ben continues.

"Mother—" Percival says.

"Three!" Big Ben says as he swings the door open to see the double barrel shotgun staring at him.

BOOM!!

The blast is so powerful, it knocks Big Ben up in the air and he's dead before he hits the ground. Lee pushes his way in the apartment and now barks in perfect English, "Ching Chow this, motherfucker!!"

In the bedroom, the shotgun blast makes Percival and Woody jump. Smiley smiles slightly as Percival is distracted and lowers his gun. He takes out his knife and stabs Percival in the neck and then reaches for the gun. In the middle of the struggle, the gun goes off and hits Woody in the chest, and he falls to the ground. Smiley rushes to his side and holds his face. "Woody?? Woodrow??" Smiley pleads with desperation and watches as Woody slumps over and dies. Percival puts his hand on his neck to stop the bleeding and looks on in horror at what he's done. His mouth is open as he lowers his gun completely. Smiley looks menacingly at Percival who starts to slowly back away. Smiley reaches for Percival's hand with the gun and breaks his wrist causing him to drop the gun. He picks up the gun and presses it to Percival's forehead. "Let me show you how it's done." He pulls the trigger killing Percival.

Smiley leaves the bedroom and sees the door to the other bedroom ajar. He opens it a little more and sees Emily gagged and tied to the chair. Emily tries to talk to Smiley, but he closes the door and leaves.

Back in the front of the apartment, Lee runs in and points his gun and Ridley who ducks under the kitchen table. Lee takes that opportunity to reload his weapon. Ridley pokes his head up and sees Lee loading his gun and shoots Lee. He drops the shells on the floor as he dies. Tom and Joanna both enter and takes shots at Ridley forcing him to run in the living room. They follow him as he bends down behind the couch. Ridley stands slightly and yells, "They're here for the girl! Kill that bitch!" ET and Mookie take their guns out and walk to the back of the apartment. Joanna pushes past Tom and yells, "No!! Emily!!" She starts firing wildly at Ridley, and one of the bullets goes through the couch and hits Ridley in the leg. "Fuck!" Ridley yells as he falls to the ground. Joanna comes around the couch to where he is and is about to fire. Ridley takes careful aim and waits until Joanna comes into view and shoots her in the chest. She falls back. Ridley slowly stands up and shoots her in the head, and she hits the floor, dead. Tom shoots Ridley in the arm causing him to drop his gun. He tries to reach for it, but Tom kicks the gun out of his reach and shoots Ridley in the shoulder. Tom then goes back to grab the shotgun Lee was carrying.

ET and Mookie are walking to the bedroom where Emily is being held. ET is walking a little faster than Mookie. As soon as ET rounds the corner, Smiley shoots him in the head with enough force that his head smacks against the adjacent wall. Mookie jumps back and says, "Shit." Smiley comes around the corner with his gun raised. Mookie sees this and turns back in the other direction for cover and starts firing wildly. As soon as Smiley sees this, he ducks for cover, smiles slightly and goes into the bedroom where Emily is.

In the bedroom, Smiley sees Emily gagged and tied up. She is still making a lot of incoherent noises. Smiley drags the chair to the door and says, "I need you for a second." Emily's eyes widen, and her body moves up and down as she is still trying to be heard and understood.

In the living room, Ridley is laying on the floor holding his shoulder while Tom comes back in the living room with the shotgun in one hand and some shells in the other. "OK Officer. I give up." Ridley says with his arms slightly raised. Tom ignores him and starts loading the gun. Ridley sees this and says, "Yo, what the fuck are you doing? Read me my rights!" Tom continues to load the gun and says, "I'm about to." Ridley gets very nervous and says, "Listen, I don't fuck around. You ain't got to worry about me snitching. I won't say shit."

"I'm not worried." Tom says as he finishes loading the gun and points both barrels in Ridley's face. His lip starts to quiver, and he says, "Y-You're a fucking cop, man. You're supposed to do the right thing."

"I am." Tom says. He fires both barrels in Ridley's face taking it clean off.

In the bedroom, Mookie slowly moves toward the door. He tries to open it but can't. He uses his shoulder as a battering ram to open the door, but it doesn't budge. He kicks the door to get it to open. After a few minutes, Mookie forces the door open after hearing a crash. He goes inside and sees Emily still tied to the chair and still gagged. He takes the gag off.

"Well, it's about fucking time!" Emily yells. "He used the chair to brace up against the door?" Mookie asks. "Of course, he fucking did! Get me out of here!" Emily responds. Mookie looks around the room and asks, "Is he still here? Where is he now?" Emily looks him in the eye and says, "Where do you fucking think?" Mookie focuses on the closet. He slowly moves closer and listens for any noise. He presses his head against the door when suddenly two gunshots pierce through. Mookie is only able to fire back once before falling to the ground. He is still moving slightly when Smiley slowly opens the door and lands on his knees holding his side. He spits out some blood and looks over at Mookie. Smiley reaches for a gun and slowly stands up. He walks over to Mookie, points the gun to his head and pulls the trigger. He exchanges looks with Emily and leaves.

In the living room, Tom checks on Ridley's body to make sure he's dead. He then looks at Joanna and Lee and sees they are also dead. He takes a deep breath and slowly gets up and yells, "Smiley! You alive back there?" He starts to walk towards the back when he sees Smiley coming towards him. Tom smiles slightly and says, "Now that everyone's dead, the first thing we have to do is—"

Smiley shoots Tom once in the shoulder and once in the leg. "AHHHHH!!!" Tom screams in pain. "What the fuck are you doing?" Tom asks while yelling at the top of his lungs. "I'm doing you a favor." Smiley responds. Tom shoots wildly at Smiley, but he misses. Tom sees Smiley smiles slightly at him and walks to the back bedrooms. He tries to stand up but can't put too much pressure on his leg. Tom hears noise coming from the back of the apartment. He listens very carefully.

"Come here bitch!! This is all your fault!!" Smiley yells.

"No, Smiley!! Please!!!" Emily pleads. Tom then hears a cracking sound and two gunshots. He gasps and says, "Fuck!" Tom struggles to get up and tries in vain to move as fast as he can. He falls in pain but continues to crawl toward Emily. He now hears breaking glass. "You motherfucker!" Tom screams. "Emily!!!" He screams with fear and desperation. Tom uses the wall as a crutch and stands up and limps and hops over to Emily. He finds her on the floor with a deep gash on her head still tied to the chair. Tom looks over and sees a trail of blood leading to the broken window. He also sees the bags of money are gone. As the faint sounds of sirens are heard in the distance, Tom unties Emily and cradles her head in his lap. "Emily, can you hear me? Please don't die." Tom says in a very soft voice. Emily moans. Tom looks down at her and asks, "Emily??" She moans again. Tom brushes the blood-soaked hair out of her face and says, "Everything is going to be alright. The police are here. The police are here." The sirens get louder and louder. Tom looks at Emily, the blood on the floor and the broken glass and shakes his head.

Chapter Twelve

Tom is now in a hospital bed. He has an IV hooked up to one arm and his injured arm in a sling. Standing around his bed are Detectives Baker, Gibbons, Lars, and Captain Dennis. "So, when did they abduct Emily?" Dennis asks. Tom thinks for a moment, then says, "It must have been sometime during the day. Her mother came to my house badly beaten and raped. They told her the girl would die if the money weren't returned."

"And during the shootout, they were all killed." Dennis says. Tom looks away and says, "That's correct." Dennis rubs his eyes then says, "Sorry, Tom but I want to go back for a minute. How long have you been working with this Smiley person?

"A while. I arrested him some time ago, and he told me things that quite honestly, I couldn't believe." Tom says. Lars looks over at everyone and says, "Like Jason being Clayton." Gibbons shakes his head and says, "I still can't get over that shit."

Baker takes a step forward and says, "So, during that bust a while back and we were looking for Smiley, you did get him out, didn't you?" Tom looks Baker in the eye and says, "I did. Your snitch Angel was targeted for assassination."

"Really?" Dennis asks. "You knew he was a snitch?"

Tom smiles slightly and says, "Everyone knew he was a snitch." "So why keep from us?" Baker asks very defensively.

Tom looks at Baker and says, "Russell and I had more than one conversation leading me to believe there were other cops on Clayton's payroll. I didn't know who to trust." Dennis looks at Tom and asks, "Really? The hole ran that deep?"

Tom shrugs his shoulders and says, "Don't take my word for it. Just ask Russell. He can verify everything I've said. He's still on suicide watch, right?" All of the cops look at each other and Tom looks confused. Baker puts his hand on Tom's shoulder and says, "Well, he was on suicide watch until this morning when they found him dead in his cell." Tom's eyes get very wide, and his mouth slightly opens. "What?? When? How?" Tom asks.

Baker says, "Every person on suicide watch gets checked on every fifteen minutes. Right after his last check, he swallowed his tongue and was dead at the next check. Tom shakes his head at hearing this news. Dennis moves closer to his bed and says, "Tom, I have to be honest with you. Baker had a suspicion you and Smiley were working together. He thought you guys were hitting drug dealers or stealing money from somewhere. Maybe Ridley found out you stole from him and kidnapped the girl for ransom or something."

Tom sits up and asks, "How is she by the way?" Dennis smiles a little and says, "She's fine. I was thinking about launching an investigation, but I've decided against it. Tom looks a little shocked and asks, "Why is that?"

Dennis sits in the chair next to his bed and says, "Well, for starters you saved the girl, recovered some drug money from Ridley's apartment, you uncovered the identity of a major drug dealer we've been looking for and you did all of this just months before you retire." Lars smiles and says, "Talk about going out with a bang."
"Besides, usually when a drug dealer and a cop are working together, it would not be beneficial for that dealer to shoot the cop." Dennis continues. Tom looks very confused by that statement and asks, "What are you saying?" Baker says, "He's

saying Smiley did you a favor by shooting you." Dennis leans forward in the chair and asks, "Why did he shoot you?"

Tom looks up for a minute, then says, "I told him he would do very little jail time once this was over." They all look very confused. "I had to tell him something to get him to keep helping me. I wanted him to verify the story and get something on record. He initially said yes, but as we got closer to the end he got very nervous. There was a struggle, and he shot me trying to get away. There was a trail of blood going out of the windows of one of the back bedrooms.

"Well, that'll make him easy to find." Dennis says. Lars moves toward Dennis and says, "We have to search every ER in the Bronx and parts of lower Westchester. Did he tell you his real name? It can't be Smiley." Tom turns to Lars and says, "He never told me. One condition he had to working with me was never knowing his government name. Lars takes out a pad and pen and asks, "What was he wearing?" Tom laughs for a bit and says, "Thug shit. A pair of jeans that fit way too big with no belt, of course, a black hoodie and a baseball cap with The Boogie Down written on it." Baker smiles to himself and says, "I just don't understand why they were their pants like that."

"Seriously. How much does a belt cost?" Lars asks. Gibbons starts laughing and says, "You ever see them try to run holding up their pants? Funniest shit ever!" All of the cops laugh. Once the laughter dies down, Dennis says, "OK, let's search for this asshole before he gets out of the city."

Tom's eyes get wide, he snaps his fingers and says, "He did tell me he had someone waiting for him under the bridge. I assume it's the GWB." Dennis says, "Well, let not assume anything. Let's search every bridge in and out of New York. Let's also lock down the area and search every car and truck and checkpoints all over the Bronx. Let's not take any chances."

"How long do you think it'll take to catch him?" Tom asks. Dennis stands up and says, "It won't take long at all. We'll fucking catch him. You know why? Because they still haven't figured out what we've known for years."

"And what's that?" Tom asks.

Baker takes a step closer and says, "If you dress and act a certain way, people make assumptions about you. You wear baggy pants and a backward cap, don't be fucking surprised when the cops stop you." Gibbons chuckles a little and says, "Yeah, but those assholes need to play the tough guy shit for the streets."

"If they dressed better, they'd be impossible to see." Lars says. Tom laughs loudly at this. So loud, the officers stop speaking and look at him. "What the hell is so funny, man?" Lars asks. Tom stops laughing a little and says, "Can you imagine a guy like Smiley wearing a fifteen-hundred-dollar suit?" All of the cops and laughing. "With a copy of the New York Times with him? He'd walk right past us, and we'd never know." Baker says. All of the cops laugh hard.

"OK. Everybody out. I need to speak to Tom alone." Dennis says. All of the cops are gone, and Dennis locks the door. He walks back over to Tom's bed and says, "Going out with a bang, huh?" Tom smiles slightly and says, "Yeah, something like that." Dennis moves closer to Tom and says, "You're not supposed to know this, but you're being promoted. With this higher pay scale, your retirement pension will be outstanding."

"Thanks. I appreciate that." Tom says. "That job at the academy is waiting for you after you retire." Dennis says. He then moves closer to Tom and says, "And, uhh we're handling that other situation for you."

Tom sits up in his bed and says, "Tell me again, what happened? Sabrina was driving?"

Dennis takes a deep breath and says, "Amy was trying to teach Sabrina how to drive. She blocked the crosswalk, so Sabrina backed up. But she forgot the car was still in reverse when the light changed; she banged right into the woman crossing the street behind her. We have six witnesses who took pictures of the license plate and eight people who identified Sabrina as the driver and Amy as the passenger."

"Who'd she hit?" Tom asks. Dennis goes to sit back down and says, "This is where the story gets interesting. The woman's name is Guadalupe Maria De Santos from Honduras. She and her husband came here illegally when they were teenagers where they settled in Texas. Five years and three kids later, everything is going great until one night the husband gets caught up in a bar brawl he didn't even start. He knew the cops were coming for him so to protect his family he had his car parked a few blocks away. When the cops came, he led them on a foot chase to his car where he then led them on a high-speed chase heading west." Tom looks a little confused and asks, "Why West?"

"Because his wife and kids had another car waiting for them to go East. Once he found out they were safe, he gave up. He was arrested, tried, convicted and incarcerated. After he got out, he was deported. Guadalupe and they kids settled in the Bronx where they stayed under the radar for thirty-seven years." Dennis says.

Tom lets his mouth slide open from the shock. "Thirty-seven years? What did she do for work?" He asks. Dennis sits back and says, "She worked as a cleaning lady. Cleaning people's homes all over the Bronx and parts of Westchester. She was able to put her kids through college. One is a doctor, one's a pharmacist, and the last one is a lawyer. An immigration lawyer." Tom rolls his eyes and says, "Oh shit."

"Yup." Dennis says. "And when she got out of surgery, that was the first call she made." He continues. Tom sits there for a few seconds and says, "I'm surprised I haven't seen it on the news yet."

"You probably won't." Dennis says. "She and her husband applied for citizenship when the kids were small because their biggest fear was being separated from them. After his arrest, the applications process was put on hold. But because of what happened to her, things have to be revisited. So we made a deal."

"What kind of deal?" Tom asks.

Dennis sits up in the chair and says, "She won't press charges, and we'll fast track her application and she'll be a US Citizen by the end of the week." Tom smiles for a bit then says, "What ever happened to the husband?"

Dennis laughs a little and says, "Not sure. For all we know, he could have snuck back in the country, and they could still be together. Who knows and who cares. The point is, she didn't want to risk being separated from her kids and we didn't want the scandal of the wife and daughter of one of the most decorated officers in the department to be arrested. Brass wants this taken care of quickly and quietly." Tom sits there for a minute and says, "I don't know what to say."

Dennis looks around the room and says, "Speaking of which, have they shown up yet? Amy and Sabrina I mean?" Tom shakes his head 'no.' There is a very uncomfortable silence, and Dennis finally says, "Well, I'm sure they will get here soon. Get some rest. I'll talk to you later." Dennis unlocks the door and leaves.

Tom sits there for a few minutes, and there is a knock at the door. Tom checks the time and mumbles, "Well, it's about fucking time, Amy." He adjusts himself and yells, "Come in!" The door slowly opens, and Baker walks in. Tom is shocked, and his eyes widen. "Baker?" he says. "You forgot something?"

Baker moves slowly toward him and says, "I don't want to take up to much of your time. I know you've been through a lot. I want to apologize for some of the things I said. For me to even suggest that you—"

"Baker, there's no need for that." Tom says cutting him off. "Yes, there is." Baker continues. "You are a legend in the department, and I'm ashamed for even mentioning it to you. I hope they're no hard feelings." Baker extends his hand. Without hesitation, Tom gives Baker a firm handshake and says, "Like it never happened." Baker leaves, and Tom sits there alone. He is smiling to himself.

*

Police officers are going in every Bronx area hospital emergency room looking for Smiley. They walk in the X-Ray room and they even, while wearing surgical scrubs, demand access to the operating theater to see if Smiley is on the table. They can't find him.

Police also set up checkpoints all over the Bronx and on every bridge in the tri-state area. They search every car and passenger in it. They still can't find him.

*

After Smiley broke the windows, he climbed out and down the fire escape. With both bags on his back, Smiley runs as fast and as far as he could. He runs down Briggs Ave to One hundred and ninety-eighth street. Smiley then runs across the Grand Concourse until he gets to Creston Avenue. Once there, he hears the sirens coming from Briggs Ave. He continues to run and walk very fast. He checks his gunshot wound and sees he is losing a lot of blood. He takes out his phone to call the Doctor. "I had a feeling you'd be calling me." The doctor says. "Red Rover. Red Rover. Meet me at Harris Park." Smiley says and hangs up.

In the doctor's house, he grabs his medical bag and runs out of the house. In his garage, he gets in a huge SUV and takes off.

When he gets to Harris Park, he finds Smiley hiding by lying next to a few homeless people on the bench and bleeding heavily. He looks around and sees no one. Smiley opens his eyes. He sees the doctor and the vehicle he drove in. He smiles and says, "Is there enough room?" The doctor smiles back and says, "Of course there is." They both look up and sees a police helicopter canvassing the area and moving closer to where they are. They look at each other as the doctor helps Smiley up and walks him over to the SUV.

The doctor is driving towards the highway and sees a police roadblock up ahead. He stomps on the floor twice. When it's his turn, several armed police officers surround the car. Some of the officers shine their light in the back seats and sees he is the only passenger.

"Where you are going?" the lead officer asks.

"Home. I live in Yonkers." The doctor responds back.

"Open the back." The officer demands. The doctor unlocks it. Several of the cops converge to the back door with their hands on their guns. They open the door and find no one there. Once they give the car the all clear, they let him go. The doctor gets on the highway and drives home.

Once he gets to his house, he drives in his garage to park. Once the garage door closes, the doctor gets out, opens the back door and lifts the seat in the second row and helps Smiley out of the car. The doctor grabs a nearby wheelchair and sits a limp Smiley on it. The doctor pushes him into a room which is a makeshift operating theater. The doctor lays Smiley on the table and cuts him out of his clothes. He first gives Smiley blood through an IV. Then, after sterilizing the gunshot wound, the doctor slowly and carefully starts to take the bullet fragments out of him. Once all of the bullet fragments are out, Smiley is stitched up, and he rests.

Sometime later, Smiley walks in the kitchen and sees the Doctor having a drink. He also sees a plate of food waiting for him.

Smiley walks over to the doctor and asks, "How long have I been out?" The doctor stands up and asks, "Where's your key?" Smiley give him a key and follows the doctor to a large steel door that leads to the basement. They enter the basement, and the doctor turns the lights on, Smiley sees a row of similar looking lockers with name tags on them. They read, Ridley, Big Ben, Boozer, Smiley, Fozzy, and Menace. The names of Fozzy and Boozer have already been crossed out. "You can cross out Ridley and Big Ben too." Smiley says. The doctor crosses those name out. "Who's Menace?" Smiley asks.

The doctor takes the key Smiley gave him and opens his locker. He takes out a change of clothes and another bag. Smiley opens the other bag and sees a lot of different fake documents including drivers ID, passport and birth certificate. While he is inspecting these, the doctor says, "You've been out for about three hours. You need to eat, shower, change and go. You know the rules. Use the shower next to the garage. The doctor goes back upstairs.

Afterward, Smiley walks into the living room from the kitchen wiping his mouth and wearing a new set of clothes. "The old ones are near the furnace. Make sure you burn them completely." He says to the doctor

"I know what I need to do." The doctor responds. He takes out pain pills and places them on the table. "For the pain. You need to rest for a while." The doctor says. "How long is a while?" Smiley asks. "A few months at least. You lost a lot of blood, and you have significant tissue damage. The body needs time to heal." The doctor says. Smiley takes out some money and places it on the table. "Looks a little light." The doctor says.

Smiley takes out his gun and says, "I could have been out the state hours ago. You fucking call me and drag me back into this shit? You're lucky I don't shoot you." The doctor raises his hands a little and says, "You called me, remember! Besides,

you shot a fucking cop! What the fuck was I supposed to do?"
Smiley puts his gun away, picks up his bags and leaves.
Outside of his house, Smiley take out his phone dials and says,
"Be ready for me. I'll be there in thirty to forty minutes." He
hangs up.

*

Benjamin and Preeti are sitting in the living room watching the
news of how a cop named Tom Sims was shot earlier that night
and police are on the hunt for the shooter. The news report also
asks people not to go outside unless it is absolutely mandatory.
Outside of their apartment, they can hear police sirens and
helicopters in the area. Benjamin's phone rings but he doesn't
recognize the number. He gets up and goes to an isolated part
of the house.

"Who is this?" Ben asks. "Remember me? We met not too long
ago when the car Horace was driving stalled." Smiley says in a
very sinister tone. Ben covers the phone and asks, "How the
fuck did you get my number?"

"Take a wild guess." Smiley says. Benjamin thinks for a minute
then his body posture falls. "Those fucking idiots." He says. "I
need you to pick me up and drop me off somewhere." Smiley
says.

Benjamin covers the phone and says, "I'm not doing a
motherfucking thing."

"I'm giving you twenty minutes to pick me up on the corner of
Waring and Bronx Park East or your pregnant woman is dead."
Smiley says. "How did fuck did you—" Ben says before
stopping.

"And it won't be right away. I know where you live and I'll wait for the right moment. She'll never fucking see me coming. You now have nineteen minutes and ten seconds." Smiley says and hangs up. Ben hangs up the phone and checks the time. "Shit." He says to himself. He slowly walks back in the living room to Preeti who asks, "Who was that?"

"I have to go out." Benjamin says very defeated. She sits up in the chair and says, "What? Why?" Ben walks over and grabs his tools and says, "Someone is having car trouble. I need to take a look. I have to." Preeti gets up and walks him over to the front door. "I really wish you wouldn't, but I know you have to. You have your phone?" Benjamin takes it out and shows it to her. They kiss, and he leaves.

Outside, he looks around for people and a street camera. He doesn't see any, so he goes to an older car and takes out his slim Jim metal rod and sliding it in and out of the driver's side window to get it open. Once inside, he rips off the panel to the steering wheel revealing lots of wires. He takes certain wires and twists them together to get the engine started.

He drives to the corner of Waring and Bronx Park East and waits there. Smiley comes from around one of the stone pillars at the entrance of the park with the bags. Smiley loads all of his bags in the back seat and gets in. He takes his gun out and points it to Benjamin's head.

"Take Waring all the way down." Smiley says. Benjamin starts driving. "Those assholes told you where I live?" he asks. Smiley is constantly looking out of the window for police. "How are you planning on getting out? You told that cop you had someone waiting for you under the bridge. That wasn't very smart." Smiley glances at him and says, "Of course it was."

"How? They have every bridge covered." Benjamin says. Smiley smiles slightly at him and says, "Not every bridge."

"Go towards Orchard." Smiley says. Benjamin takes the streets toward Orchard Beach. They are coming up on a sign that reads for Orchard Beach, keep going straight and for City Island, turn right. Benjamin is in the lane to go straight. "Turn right." Smiley says. Benjamin turns back a little and says, "You said you're going to Orchard." Smiley grimaces in pain and presses the gun to his head and says, "Fucking turn right. Head to City Island."

Benjamin heads towards City Island. Right before he gets to the City Island bridge, Smiley says, "Slow down. Slow down." Benjamin looks around and says, "Shit."

"I don't see any cops. Do you?" Smiley asks. "Stop here and put your hazard lights on." He continues. Smiley gets out, and a man in a small motorboat under the bridge emerges. He helps Smiley load up his boat. Smiley tries to load up the other large bag of money. "We can't take it. It'll be too heavy." The man says. Smiley looks at Benjamin and says, "Give me your phone." Benjamin gives it to him. Smiley points to the bag and says, "You keep this one for now. I'll come back for it later. Remember, I'm watching you." The man helps Smiley in the boat, and they cast off. Smiley lies under a tarp as they travel North on the Long Island Sound, Smiley peeks out and sees the many police lights on the Throggs Neck Bridge in the distance. He smiles to himself and goes back under the tarp.

Benjamin slowly drives across the City Island Bridge looking in the distance at the police lights. He parks in front of a fire hydrant and sits there.

Sometime later, Smiley is driving down the highway, and he passes a sign that says 'Welcome to North Carolina.' He continues to drive until he sees the town named 'Roper.' Smiley pulls into a seedy, filthy looking motel. He goes inside and sees the desk clerk. The clerk is a young dirty looking man who looks very shocked to see Smiley. "Where the hell have you been? You were supposed to be here months ago."

"I needed extra time to rest. Doctor's orders." Smiley says with reserved sarcasm. The clerk leans toward Smiley and says, "He's been waiting for you, and he knows what's been happening in the Bronx. First with you and then with that whole Eagle Car thing."

Smiley smiles and says, "Yeah. I saw that on the news. That was wild."

"Anyway, he said he's going to turn you over for the reward. He paid me extra to give him a heads up when you finally showed up. I was hoping you would give me a little extra on top of the extra for giving you the heads up." The clerk says while looking away. Smiley gives him the once over and slowly goes into his bag and hands out a small stack of bills. "Not a word that I'm here." Smiley says. The clerk is counting the money and says, "I'm sorry sir. Who are you?"

"What's his name again?" Smiley asks. "Nimal Ha-hap—I can't fucking pronounce it. He always says pronouncing his last name was painful. He's in room eight. What're gonna do now?" The clerks asks. Smiley looks around for a moment, then sees the housekeeping closet behind the clerk and smiles.

Inside of the slightly dingy motel room, Nimal Hapuarachi is sitting on the bed flipping channels. The room is pretty dank looking with a huge window near the front door. He is a young Indian man in his late thirties. He has thick black hair slicked back and a large ring on his pinky finger. He also has several long cuts on both sides of his face that could have only been made by a very sharp knife. He continues to flip the channels until he sees a story of Preeti and Dhack Winston on television. The images show them walking down the street at night together as the crowd cheers them on. Both Preeti and Dhack look very uncomfortable. Nimal smiles at seeing her. When Preeti is shown to be pregnant, Nimal drops his smile. He takes out his phone and calls her. "Hey girl, I'm watching you on TV, and I gotta say you looking pretty fucking good. You also looking pretty fucking pregnant. I don't know who the father is, but it ain't me. It should be me cause last I checked, I was your fucking husband."

While Nimal is speaking, there is a knock at his door. He reaches for his gun and looks through the window. He sees the housekeeping cart roll near. Nimal puts the gun down and gets up to open it. While doing so, he says on the phone, "You need to call me back and let me know who the fuck—" As soon as he opens the door, Smiley pounces on him pistol whipping him. "Pree—" Nimal says as he tries to fight back. Smiley gets him in a chokehold on the bed and begins to strangle him. Smiley is breathing very heavily as he slowly kills Nimal. He tries to fight back until his body moves less and less until it stops moving altogether. Once Smiley is sure Nimal is dead, he gathers all of the fake documents and money and starts to leave. Smiley notices the phone on the bed. Still trying to catch his breath, he slowly walks over and picks it up. He holds the phone close to his ear but says nothing. Smiley hangs up, takes the phone with him and leaves.

Epilogue

At the end of the school year where Percival attended, members of the media are in front of the school along with dozens of his family, friends, and teachers. They are all holding balloons. Among the crowd of people are Melanie and Mr. Beecher. He looks particularly heartbroken and wipes tears from his face. Percival's mother Gladys is also there with tears in her eyes. At the same time, all of the balloons are released, and the crowd erupts in claps, tears, and hugs. Gladys is hugging several members of the school staff and students. Melanie wraps her arms around Gladys very tightly and cries in her arms. Gladys is a little taken aback by this. "I loved your son. And he loved me." Melanie says. Gladys looks her very perplexed. After Melanie lets Gladys go, she goes to talk to members of the media. Gladys looks across the street and sees Murdock standing there. They make eye contact, and Murdock walks away. A reporter comes over to her and says, "Tell me. How are you feeling after seeing this heartfelt display to your son?" Gladys looks around at the many people there. Melanie manages to move right next to Gladys. She adjusts her hair a little. Gladys looks around and says, "This is all very nice. I am very grateful to the people who came out to pay tribute to my son who was, despite what was reported, was a true victim of circumstance. I wonder how many of the people here truly knew my son." She stares at Melanie who sheepishly avoids eye contact and slinks in the background. Gladys walks away and follows Murdock who is sitting at the same picnic table under the tree where he and Percival had their encounter. Gladys sits next to him.

"I didn't see you over there with everybody else." Gladys says. Murdock rolls his eyes and states, "The school didn't do this in his memory. They did it for the money. This was a dog and pony show so the school can go to the heads of education and ask for more funding. This was a three ringed circus. They probably told certain people to show up and show emotion, and later there'll be a pizza party or some shit." Gladys looks at him and says, "I never thought about it that way. You're pretty smart." Murdock laughs and says, "Percy thought so. He thought I was brilliant but also very lazy. I was wasting my potential."

"What do you think?" Gladys asks.

"I think he was right. I need to get off my ass and apply myself." Murdock says.

Gladys reaches for Murdock's hand and says, "I'd like to talk to you more about Percy. I thought I knew him well but apparently not well enough. Will you tell me what you knew about him? What he was really like?" Murdock grabs her hand and replies, "Of course. Anytime."

"Did the police tell you what happened to him?" Murdock asks.

"All I know is a man named Smiley shot him." Gladys replies. Murdock rubs his chin and asks, "Who's that?" Gladys shrugs her shoulders and replies, "Don't know and don't care to. But I will find this man and do everything in my power to kill him."

"And I will do everything in my power to help you." Murdock responds with tears in his eyes.

"Can I buy you breakfast? Are you hungry?" Gladys asks.

"Starving." Murdock says. They both get up and walk off together while school officials talk to members of the media.

*

In the city of Los Angeles, there is a premiere of an art exhibit. The gallery is being held in a huge room with white walls, floors and high ceilings. The only colors are from photos of flowers, highways, insects, buildings, etc. Tara, an exquisite and beautiful looking blond-haired blue-eyed woman walks over to Smiley as he stands in front of a picture of Percival right before he threatened to shoot him. Percival's face is one of shock, fright, and horror. The look is mesmerizing. "You must be Tom." Ana says extending her hand. Smiley shakes it and says, "I must be."

"I'm Tara." She says grinning from ear to ear. "My pleasure Tara." Smiley says back. Tara then turns to the photo. "Fascinating. The look on his face is just haunting. How did you ever get him to give you that expression so vividly?" She asks. Smiley stares at the photo for a bit then says, "Well, I told him to imagine he and two of his friends are in a room with a deranged sociopath. He's already killed the two, and you're next. He thought about it for a minute, and this is the face he gave me."

"Wow. That's just masterful." Tara says. "Well, he did all the work. I was just there to capture the moment." Garrett walks over. He is a very handsome blond-haired blue-eyed man. "This is my brother Garrett." Tara says. He and Smiley shake hands. "Would you like a drink?" Garrett asks.

"I would love one. Anything but Vodka." Smiley says. "Me too. I'll get them." Tara says very enthusiastically. "I'll be right back." She leaves. Garrett is looking at the picture while Smiley is staring at him for a bit. Smiley turns his attention to the picture. Garrett, still staring at the photo says, "My sister finds you very intriguing."

Smiley also staring at the photo and replies, "I know. She's been staring at me from the left side of the room for twelve minutes."

Garrett then turns to Smiley and says, "I also find you very intriguing." "I know. You've been staring at me from the right side of the room for twenty-two minutes." Smiley says while still staring at the photo. "I did some checking on you." Garrett says. Smiley slowly turns to him and asks, "Did you now? What did you find out?"

"I know about the carjacking in North Carolina and how you had to get away so you came out West." Garrett says. Smiley smiles slightly and says, "I wanted a safer environment."

"So, you came to LA?" Garrett replies with a chuckle and a broad smile. Smiley shrugs his shoulders and says, "Seemed like a good idea at the time." Garrett circles Smiley and says, "What I don't know is who funded this exhibition for you." Smiley circles him back and replies, "My benefactor prefers to remain anonymous." They stop circling, face each other and Garrett says, "First time in a new city and an unknown photographer can secure funds for this elaborate affair. That's a very useful tool."

Smiley looks at Garrett up and down and says, "I have a lot of useful tools." Garrett winks at Smiley when Tara comes over with drinks for everyone. They take their glasses. Tara says, "A toast." They all raise their glasses.

"To your opening." Tara says with a smile.

"To your opening." Garrett says with a smile.

They all clink their glasses and have a sip.

Tara looks at Smiley and says, "I hate to put you on the spot, but you have such a wonderful smile. I think I'll call you smiley from now on. Has anyone ever called you that?"

Smiley turns to her and says, "I do believe you are the first." They clink their glasses again and take a sip.

*

Back in Manhattan, on a very sunny afternoon, Tom is standing in front of the main building for Ivan & Duke, the largest and most well-known law firm in the country. There's not a cloud in the sky, and there are lots of people out and about all over the city. Tom is staring at the crowd when his lawyer walks outside of the building in a huff with a scowl on his face. He stands directly in front of Tom. Tom looks at him and says, "Thanks for helping me out back there." The lawyer is taken aback by that statement. He takes a step back in amazement. "Help you out?" he says with frustration. "You gave her everything! The house, all the money in the bank and the car." He continues. Tom continues to stare at the people and says, "Yeah, but she can never touch my pension as a condition of getting everything else. That belongs to me."

The lawyer rubs his face and ponders, "I wonder why she never tried to take it."

"She knows why." Tom mumbles under his breath. The lawyer shakes his head and walks away. A few minutes later Amy walks out of the building looking very upset. She storms over to Tom and says, "Thank you. Thank you for ruining my life. After all I've done for you." Tom turns to her and says, "You mean like putting pressure on me to break the law? Thank you for visiting me in the hospital after I got shot. I appreciate it."

Amy turns away sheepishly and replies, "You know how I feel about hospitals. Especially after my mother died."

"Cry me a fucking river. Now you can spend all the money you want." Tom says. "I know you're holding out on me." Amy says while wagging her finger in his face.

Tom gets in her face and says, "I told you that money was never for me. I wanted to save the girl." Amy looks around and asks, "And where the fuck is she now? You think you'll ever see her again? What about me? What the fuck do I get?"

"I gave you the house now sell it. Since Russell killed himself, Debbie can use the company. Maybe you can move in with her out on Long Guyland. Just make sure they're no Blacks or Albanians in the area. Just good old fashion white folks, right?" Tom barks at her. Her mouth opens a little at what he just said. "How can you be so insensitive. So mean?" Amy pleads.

Tom gets in her face and says, "I had practice from all the years I was married to you."

Amy steps back. She looks away and says, "I guess I should thank you for not reporting that accident. Is it true the woman was illegal?"

"It is. Been in the country for over thirty years and raised three kids while cleaning houses for a living. She's a model citizen." Tom says. Amy huffs and replies, "But she's not an actual citizen. Technically she should be kicked out of my country." Tom huffs right back and retorts, "And technically, you and Sabrina should be locked up for nearly killing the woman and fleeing the scene of an accident."

Amy looks around embarrassed and says, "Keep your fucking voice down." "What's the matter?" Tom says. You're embarrassed to speak loudly in your own country?"

"Sabrina was driving you know." Amy says.

"Yes, I know. They told me." Tom says.

"She'll hate you forever; you know that? Amy asks. Tom looks at her up and down and says, "For what? For divorcing you? You turned her against me years ago. This won't make a difference." Amy sucks her teeth and walks away. Tom watches her walks down the street. He looks at her until she is out of sight then turns and walks away.

Tom continues to walk down the street until he reaches the train station. He takes the uptown six train to the last stop which is Pelham Bay Park. Tom walks in the park and sees Emily sitting on a bench. She has scars on her face from the earlier attack. She also has two large backpacks next to her. Emily looks up at Tom and says, "You're late. I should sue."

"I have nothing left but my integrity." Tom says with a slight smile. He sits next to her, and she asks, "How'd it go?" Tom lets out a deep sigh and says, "I got what I expected."

"You didn't want to house? Even after you fixed it up?" Emily asks. Tom shakes his head 'no' and says, "All done with ill-gotten gains. No thank you. My conscience is clear."

"Are you happy?" She asks. Tom takes a deep breath and says, "I'm relieved. Now I can start over." He looks around at the people in the park, then turns to Emily and says, "You wanted to meet me here. What's up?"

"This is for you." Emily says. She hands him one of the backpacks. "What's this?" Tom asks. Emily looks straight ahead, and Tom opens the bag a little and sees stacks of hundred-dollar bills strapped together. He closes the bag and looks around. Tom glares at Emily and asks, "What the hell is this?"

"Before I sold the laundromat, I did one final sweep of the place. Behind a fake wall, I found a rice bag filled with money." Emily says.

"Where did this all come from?" Tom asks.

Emily looks at the floor and says, "I heard stories about my mom, but I never believed any of them until now." Tom places the bag closer to Emily to says, "You know I can't accept this, right?"

"This isn't a bribe or a payoff. It's a gift. You saved my life." Emily says. Tom looks at the bag again and asks, "How much is here?" "Somewhere in the neighborhood of seven hundred and fifty thousand dollars." Emily responds.

"That's a very respectable neighborhood." Tom says almost awkwardly. "But this is way too much money to take from you. Take some. I insist." He continues. Emily puts her hand on the other bag and says, "Actually, I have the same amount in this bag."

Tom's eyes get wide, and his mouth gapes open. "What?" Emily asks. Tom stands up and looks around. Emily also stands up and looks straight in his eyes. "What?" She asks again.

He moves close to her and says through gritted teeth, "Each bag has the same amount?" Emily nods 'yes.' "You carried a million and a half dollars in the Bronx in broad daylight? You out of your fucking mind?" Emily moves closer to him and says, "Look around you." Tom looks around the park and sees no one is paying them any attention. "Looks at me. I'm Asian. They probably think these are textbooks or some shit."

Tom laughs loudly then covers his mouth. "Sorry for laughing." He says.

"You're supposed to laugh. It's funny." Emily says with a smile.

"So, what now?" Tom asks. Emily looks around the park then looks up at the sky then says, "Breakfast. Would you like to have breakfast with me?"

"Sure." Tom says.

"Cool." Emily says back after a pause.

They both grab their respective bags and head out of the park. "Now that you're retired, are you taking that job at the academy?" Emily asks. "I will. But first I wanted to take some time off to travel. I never got a chance to do that. What about you?" Tom responds.

"I'll go back to school." Emily says. "After my dad died, I had to drop out to help my mom. But now I can re-enroll and finish my degree." She continues. "What were you studying?" Tom asks.

"Political Science." She responds back. "What school?" He asks. "SUNY Geneseo." Emily says. "Where the hell is that?" Tom asks.

..iles and says, "Over three hundred miles away from ..gie down." Tom laughs and says, "You probably need a ..o get around up there."

"Getting a car is easy. I need to get my license first." Emily says.

"I can help you with that." Tom replies. Emily turns to Tom and asks, "You'll help me get my license?"

"Sure." Tom says.

"Cool." Emily says back after a pause.

THE END